THE LOVE OF
Whitney

Andrew P. LeBel

This book is for my friend David
Born Nov 8th 1964
Died Aug 26th 1991
You didn't need to kill yourself.
I could've helped.

Prologue

When I was growing up, I was told that childhood years were the magical years. I don't think that is, or ever was, true. Not after the nightmare my friend David and I lived through that snowy winter of 1978, in good ole Merrimac, Massachusetts. That year seemed to last forever. We made a vow to each other we'd never speak of it to anyone, ever. I've broken that vow.

Everyday for fifteen years I have thought about that winter and what we did.
I could never forget about the love of my life, who died in the icy waters of Cobblers Brook,
known as Sewer Lane.

1

It was my sixteenth birthday. I was walking home from the bus stop alone in the dark, sore from wrestling practice, and thinking about the presents my mother had bought for me, and the usual bullshit present I always got from my grandparents.

My best friend, David, was sitting on the church steps against the doors. He was holding a bottle of Vodka he most likely stole from his father's liquor cabinet. He walked toward me with his finger stuck in the throat of the bottle, swinging it from side to side. His knees and elbows were dirty from possibly being pushed down to the ground in a fight, or maybe he fell. I didn't know, and I didn't ask. As he walked closer to me, for some reason I noticed he seemed taller, a lot taller. That instant I felt strangely intimidated.

"What are you doing, Andy?" he asked, tossing the bottle into Mr. Shaw's rose garden across the street. "Hey, happy birthday by the way,"

"Thanks," I said surprised he even remembered. "Nothing, I'm just going home to have some cake and ice cream. Do you wanna come?"

"Yeah, sure. I'm always up for cake!"

We walked toward home, up the steep hill as we did everyday since we started taking the bus. I looked up at the broken street lights he and I smashed sometime ago, remembering all those thousands of rocks we threw, and giving each other the credit for finally hitting it.

When we walked into my front door, I could smell the burning candles my mother had just lit. Everyone started singing happy birthday, except for my father, the shitbag. He left when I was six. He figured the liquor bottle was more important than his kids.

David stood against the wall making funny faces at me until the singing stopped and then sat next to me at the dining room table. We knew David didn't get along with his father, and my house was a kind of retreat from his home life. Some days he would walk in with bruises on the side of his face. He would claim he fell down the steep stairs at his house, but we all knew the truth, especially when he wouldn't want to go home.

I blew the candles out just as the phone rang, and saw my mother quickly reaching for it before it stopped. "Hello," I heard her say from the kitchen. Then, without another word said, she hung up the phone. I knew who it was. My mother came back in the living room with her famous fake smile, holding one of those big knives you see in a horror movie. "Let me slice the cake so everyone can have an even piece," She said softly, still holding her fake smile. David was the first one waiting as though he hadn't eaten since school started last September. He looked at me as if he wanted to tell me something

"After we eat, let's go down to the cellar. I want to show you a new move on the weights," I said, making an excuse for him. He nodded.

When we went downstairs, David was fidgety and smiling at me like he had won the lottery. "Donna showed me," he said with the biggest smile on his face. Donna, the quiet girl with the biggest brown eyes and the longest brown hair in the neighborhood. She was the star of David's nightly dreams. Or so he says. He would dream of her wrapped up in his arms, stranded on an exotic island, and then wake up in a drenching sweat in the middle of the night. She was his ticket to happiness. She was his ticket to living.

"Showed you what?" I asked, knowing exactly where this conversation was going.

"She showed me her boobs," he said, and then he smiled as wide as a child getting the taste of his first lollipop. I saw in his eyes he was imagining his hands fondling them, so I had to ask.

"Did you touch 'em?"

"No, she was in the other room."

"Did she know she showed you her boobs?" I asked, knowing the answer already.

"I don't know," he said as the smile left his face.

"Maybe she knew you were there," I said, trying to make him feel better.

"Whitney was in the room with Donna the same time she was changing her shirt," He said, knowing I had a thing for Whitney.

"Whitney," I said as a smile came over my face. The dreams, the thoughts of her made me feel like I was giving the orphanage a million dollars. She was different from the other girls we knew in the neighborhood. And she was seventeen—a whole year older than David and me.

"What was Whitney doing?"
"Nothing," he said, looking down at the weights like he was lying to me.

"Who was she with?" I asked him, realizing there was more to his story than just seeing Donna's boobs.

"She was with that new kid from New York, what's his name?"

"Peter," I said, almost spitting his name. He was the other older one, the one who had a license to drive. He was eighteen and able to legally buy beer. God I hated him. I hated his name. I hated even the thought of him. Peter was the only person in the world that could make my blood boil. David must have seen the jealousy in my eyes. I didn't want to hear anything about Peter. The mention of him completely ruined my birthday, and I was about to chastise David when Mom yelled down to me that I had a visitor.

"Whitney!" I whispered to David and ran up the old wooden stairs. There she was, my love, Whitney Williams taking off her coat with her back toward me, and that slim sexy body I've wanted to hold since I discovered that girls were more than just girls. Her hair was long and silky, draped over her shoulders like a black negligee covering the length of her back. She turned around holding a dark blue, plain wrapped box and looked into my blue eyes. I smiled feeling my hands getting sweaty, wanting to hold her ever so close, gaze into her brown eyes forever, and kiss her ever-so soft lips. "Hey," she said with a soft twinkle in her eye that made me melt. I wanted to believe she had feelings for me and that's the reason she came tonight.

"Do miracles happen?" I asked myself. "Do they?"

"Happy birthday, old man," She said handing me the present with her arms straight out. I lightly pulled it from her hands, imagining for a brief moment about how life would be if I could just hold her forever. My mother and sister giggled and looked at me. David stood behind me staring at her. He knew she was beautiful, and better looking than his make-believe girlfriend Donna.

Whitney was wearing a black sleeveless dress just covering her knees, and a black pair of boots with a zipper on the side. She looked as though she came to pick me up for our first date. She nervously touched her thin gold necklace and followed it down to the neckline of her dress. Suddenly she turned her head and looked out the front door window as though she heard a strange noise. There he was, Peter, knocking at the door and waving. My mother smiled as she opened the door.

"We, well, I wanted to stop by to see you on your birthday." Whitney said, clasping her hands together, and stepped back from the door to give Peter enough room to enter. Her perfume tingled in my nose. I closed my eyes for a moment, breathing in, absorbing her very essence. I was crazy about her. I just wished she felt the same way.

"Hey," Peter said, waving his hand like the true piece of shit yuppie that he was. And then I saw him lightly put his hand on the small of Whitney's back. I cringed and fisted my hands tight. Peter was ugly to the bone. He had brown eyes, stick straight brown hair, with a slim, weak-looking body. He also had this, "I'm better than you attitude." Maybe since he was from the Big Apple, he thought he could do what he wanted and never had to worry about getting caught. That doesn't happen in the small hick towns, especially Merrimac, Massachusetts

"Hey, Peter," I said, thinking how good it would feel to punch him in the face as hard as I could. "What are you guys doing tonight?" I asked, trying to sound friendly spite of my anger.

"We're going to the movies. We thought maybe you wanted to go with us, since it's your birthday.

I looked at my mom. I wanted to go, but I

didn't know whether she would let me. I was surprised when she said, "As long as you come home after the movie is over." She handed me a five-dollar bill.

"Can David come?" I asked, turning around to see him. He was obviously trying to avoid being anywhere near Peter since he was in the kitchen when I found him.

Whitney looked at Peter, and kind of smiled. I could see she was afraid to ask. "Sure, if he wants to."

"Are you coming, David?" David looked at me and must have seen in my eyes that I really wanted him to go. No matter what, I wanted him to go. He nodded.

"Be home after the movie," my mother said again giving me a, you-better-get-your-birthday-ass-home-after-the-movie or else look on her face.

Whitney slipped into her coat, and smiled, putting her arm around me and making me melt inside as we walked out the front door. I wanted to grab her hand and hold it like we were lovers but remembered that shitbag Peter was walking behind us.

Peter parked his father's two-door Chevy Nova in the middle row of the drive-in movie theater in Haverhill, one of the last drive-in theaters in the country. Whitney sat up front with Peter. David and I sat in the back on the leather seats that had made us slide in every direction every time he turned a corner. I could smell the horny nervous sweat coming off Peter's body, and felt sick to my stomach.

"We're going to get some popcorn," I said pushing against his seat. I looked over the front seat, trying to squeeze through and saw Peter's sweaty hand on Whitney's bare leg close enough to feel her crotch. I slammed the seat forward causing Peter to bang his head hard against the steering wheel. David laughed and did the same, again slamming Peter's head as he squeezed through the door.

"Assholes!" We heard Peter scream at us. "Don't bother coming back." I looked back at him and glared as David and I walked to the snack shack. Peter's eyes glistened in the light, and something told me I should have stayed in the car.

2

David and I hitched to the town border, arriving there just after ten o' clock, hoping we would make it home before my mother called out the dogs. But then a car pulled up behind us and honked.

"Get in, dipshit!" we heard someone shout. I turned and saw that it was Peter. Whitney opened the passenger door. When I squeezed between the seats, I saw that her dress had been torn, revealing the straps of her bra, and there were bruises on both of her cheeks and a small laceration across the bridge of her nose. And I saw the terror and tears in her eyes, running down her swollen face.

"Take me home," she said to me quietly. "Take me home."

"Okay," I replied.

Peter sped down the road at the rate of speed where any inexperienced driver would lose control, and stopped at the bottom of our street. Whitney jumped out of the car and held the seat for David and me, then slammed the door shut and kicked it hard. Peter hollered at her to get in.

"Asshole!" she screamed at the top of her

lungs. "You'll pay for what you did, you piece of shit!"

Peter took off, tires squealing. We stood in the street, silent. David and I stared at Whitney as she wiped her eyes and tried to fix her dress.

"Take me home," she said again quietly and held the tips of my fingers.

"What happened to you?" I asked dropping my hand away from hers. "Did Peter . . . did he rape you?"

"Nothing, nothing happened," she said and began slowly walking toward her home. I could tell she was in pain by the gingerly way she walked. I knew what had happened and made a vow then and there that I would confront the bastard and make sure Peter would have to learn to walk all over again. I ran to Whitney and grabbed her arm before she fell. I wanted to kill Peter right here, right now. I kept my cool all the way to her house. When we got to her front door, David leaned against the telephone pole near her driveway. He didn't say a word the whole time walking Whitney home. I guess he didn't want to get involved.

I watched Whitney open the door and slowly step in. She didn't look back, she just shut the door.

"She's a hurtin' unit!" David said.

"No shit, Dick Tracy."

3

Three weeks later we celebrated our annual neighborhood winter barbecue. That year was the coldest party ever. The temperature never reached ten degrees all weekend, but still, everyone in the neighborhood helped out making hamburgers, hot-dogs, potato salad, and of course, brought lots of beer. The party was held at the Germanatta's house, in their huge heated garage, which they'd built over the summer. My neighbor, Scott's father, filled up a kiddie pool inside the garage, and floated around on a tire tube with a can of his favorite beer sitting on his belly. That year Whitney's dad took his clothes off and ran around outside in his underwear, and the neighborhood women had a contest to see who could pull his undies off first. All except for Mrs. Clancy, however. She was a single mom who asked Whitney's dad to come fix her kitchen sink. The whole neighborhood knew why she asked, including Whitney's mom. That year was fun. But Whitney never came out of her house.

The last time I saw Peter he was sporting a

pair of wooden crutches, with the thick foam ends that gave you a rash on your armpit and a nice pair of bright white shaded casts reaching up past his kneecaps. Although David and I had planned on telling Wayland "The Leg Breaker" about Peter's crime, we never had to. Apparently, Whitney's dad told him. And everyone knew who broke Peter's legs, even though Whitney's dad never mentioned a word to anyone during the wild party weekend. They all knew. Bad news travels fast in Merrimacport.

On the morning of November 7th, David and I were walking down the street in our ice floating attire. I had asked my mom to get me a pair of fishing waders for Christmas the year before, so I wouldn't freeze my ass off if, or when, I fell into the cold water. David was wearing his father's waders that were three sizes too long for him, but since he sprouted like a weed over the summer and fall, they really didn't look so bad.

We stopped in front of Whitney's house as we had done ever since we were able to roam the streets on our own and looked up at her window shaded with white lace curtains.

"Throw a rock up, and see if she's home," I said.

"My luck her father will come out and beat me up," David said. We both had heard rumors about Whitney's father beating up the old man across the street when the poor guy had accidentally smashed the side window of Whitney's dad's new car when he ran over a rock mowing the lawn. The guy went to the hospital and never came out, as far as we knew. We assumed he had died there. His wife had her groceries and her medications delivered, and rarely seen outside of the house

"Her father's not home," I said. "He must be working. Look, his car is gone."
David picked up a small rock, and tossed it up to the window and missed, hitting the old clapboard on the side of the house, causing one of the boards to fall off.

"Great stupid, now we're in trouble, for sure! Why'd you throw it so hard?" Whitney opened the window and waved, and then looked at the piece missing from the house and started to laugh.

"Hey, we're going down to Sewer Lane, do you want to come along?" I asked hoping she'd tag along, but I knew she wouldn't. She never did.

"No, I have chores to do," She told us.

"What are you doing later?" David asked.

"Nothing,"

"Come down later then," I said.

"Okay," she said and shut the window. She stood at the window a bit longer, and I studied her from below.

"Hey, look at Whitney," I nudged David. "Her boobs look bigger to you?"

"No," David said, picking up another rock, skipping it down the street, watching it bang into the turnaround island in the middle of the road.

"They look bigger to me."

We walked down to Sewer Lane and hopped from one floating hunk of ice to another trying to find one that could hold our weight. Suddenly, we saw Whitney's father struggling to climb up the muddy embankment near the mouth of the brook David and I exchanged glances. What was he doing there? Her father finally managed to get out of the brook and walked quickly to his Mercedes. He glanced at us once, and then slowly drove away.

4

Without warning, David jumped into the cold water, reaching just below the surface, and pulled up a wooden crutch.

"That's one of Peter's crutches!" I shouted, jumping off the ice into the brook. I pushed my way through the water toward David. Then I saw Peter's other crutch. David scoped out the ice-filled brook, slowly pushing the ice away with the foam part of the crutch. He pushed away a big piece of ice near the old stone bridge and found what we expected: Peter, floating face down in the icy water with his arms spread out, as though he belly flopped off the bridge. We pushed our way over to him, turned him over and saw bruises and cuts on his face. David tipped Peter's head up, and we saw a long deep slash across his neck. Peter's head moved around as though it was just barely attached to his body. David dropped Peter back into the water and jumped away as if he were on a springboard. He lost his balance, and fell under the icy, bloody water.

"What the fuck, David?" I yelled.

"What the fuck? What the fuck?" David

repeated, gaining his balance, wiping his face with his hand.

"Whitney's dad did this! He killed him!" I shouted.

"Ya think?" he screamed.

David grabbed Peter by the belt and pulled him to shore. I helped him drag him completely out of the water. Then we heard sirens blaring.

"Jesus, David, if they see us with him, they'll think we killed him."

We heard a car stop just at the bridge and looked up. It was a police cruiser. David instantly put his arms up in the air, and I followed suit.

The police officers slid down the muddy embankment holding onto a tree branch so they wouldn't fall into the cold water and told us to step away from the body. David and I stepped three steps back holding our hands up as high as we could until the older police officer told us to put our hands down. He also told us Whitney's father called the station himself and confessed to the murder and told them where the body was.
"He also mentioned we were going to find you boys here," he said, rather gently I thought.

I looked at David. He seemed as relieved as I was.

The police officers examined the body and took pictures as we stood there freezing our asses off, until my mother came down and picked us up. She yelled at both us for being down here, even though we'd been coming to Sewer Lane since we were ten years old.

As we drove by Whitney's house, we saw Whitney's dad, his shirt splattered with blood and mud, being taken out of the house in handcuffs with an officer on each side. Whitney stood on the porch with her mother. She looked at us briefly, and then put her head down. I wanted to jump out of the car and run over to her. I wanted to hold her tight, but the only thing I could do is stare at her from the rear window until we turned the corner and headed home.

When we walked into the house the phone was ringing.
My mother raced to the phone, and I heard her agreeing to something. When she hung up, she turned to David and me. "That was the police," she said. "They're coming over to ask you two some questions."

I felt nervous, for some reason, but David just shrugged as though he's done this a thousand times. When the police arrived, we were told to sit down at the kitchen table. Mom made them some coffee. The sergeant, his name was Vance he said, smiled. I guess he could sense how scared I was

"Tell me how you found the body? I mean, in what position?" Sergeant Vance asked pulling against his tight shirt.

"Face down," David said. The sergeant looked at me for confirmation, and I nodded.

"What did you do when you found the body?"

"I turned him over," David replied. Again I nodded my head.

"Do you think Mr. Williams killed your friend?"

"He's not my friend," David said.

"Okay, let me rephrase that. Do you think Mr. Williams killed Peter Cass?"

"Yes," I said out loud before David could answer.

"What about you, David?"

"Yes."

"You do understand, if we need you to come to court for a witness testimony, you'll need to come."

"Yes," David said, looking at me for agreement. I didn't say anything. I didn't have to.

"Why did he kill Peter?" I asked. Sergeant Vance looked at David and me and stroked his chin.

"No one knows why people do bad things." He said softly, and then he stood up pulling down his shirt again and looked at my mother in a sort of strange way. He walked away from us, gesturing my mother to come with him. They talked for a while near the front door, and then I saw Sergeant Vance shaking my mom's hand before he left.

5

Whitney unexpectedly came to my house the following Saturday after her father was hauled away. It was early morning, just after dawn. She quietly came up the stairs, lay down on the bed facing me, and wrapped her leg around me. The cut across the bridge of her nose was almost totally healed, and the bruises on her face had yellowed. She covered them with make up, but I could see the tint up close.

She stared into my eyes without saying anything, and then closed her eyes. I could feel her breath on my lips. I wondered if I was in heaven or if I was dreaming.

She put her arm around me, and lightly kissed the tip of my nose.

"That night we went to the movies," She whispered, slowly opening her eyes. "Peter raped me." She looked deep into my eyes, I thought maybe she wanted me to say something, I didn't. I couldn't. I just listened.

"That was the first time I've ever had sex with anyone. It hurt so bad I cried all night. Sometimes I think it was my fault he raped me because I keep thinking I led him on."

"Why are you telling me this?" I whispered.

"Because I know you care a lot about me, and I know you wouldn't hurt me like Peter did."

"Is that why your father killed Peter?" For the longest time she didn't say a word. I thought maybe she didn't want to think about it, or maybe she didn't want to answer it.

"I think I'm pregnant," she said pulling me closer, closing her eyes.

I didn't ask her any more questions after that. I was afraid to, or maybe I didn't want to. I stared at her thinking about the horror of what had happened in that car. Thinking about how much I wanted her, but not the way Peter had her.

"You're the only one I can trust," she whispered and lightly kissed me on the lips. I smiled at her and slid my hand down to the middle of her back feeling the clasp of her bra.

We lay there holding each other for a

long time. No one was home for most of the day. I think we fell asleep in each other's arms until the mid afternoon. She didn't want to do anything. She didn't want to face the fact that her family was shattered, that she'd see her father only through a Plexiglas wall.

The phone rang, waking us up. Whitney slid off the bed and answered it as if she lived there. "Yes, Mom," she said, in a bitchy tone. She muttered some more and then slammed the phone down and breathed a long heavy sigh, as though she was going to tell me she was moving far away.

"My mom is bringing me to the doctors in a few minutes," she said, looking out the window.

"Does she know you might be pregnant?"

"Yes. Your mother is home. I have to go." She reached over and gave me a big hug and a kiss, then slid her soft finger down the side of my face, looking at me as if she was never coming back and quickly went down the stairs, leaving out the back door before my mother saw her.

I lay in my bed for a few more minutes thinking of her.

My mother yelled up the stairs telling me to get my lazy ass out of bed and come down and help her with the groceries. Before I could obey, the phone rang.

"What are you doing?" David asked. He never said "hello" when he phoned, and I knew the sound of his voice.

"Nothing," I told him.

"Be down in a minute," he said and hung up the phone.

I noticed Whitney's school picture on the table as I hung up the phone. When I flipped it over I saw the words "I love you forever" written in black ink. I smiled and remembered the first kiss she gave me when we were ten years old. We were acting like a married couple sitting next to each other on her back porch when she kissed me under the soft moonlight. I kissed the picture and left it on the table. As I lazily trudged down the stairs, David walked in wearing his father's waders and holding a grocery bag. He placed it on the floor in the kitchen.

"That's the last one," he said to my mother.

"Thank you, David. At least someone around here helps out." She looked directly at me.

"Hey, go get your waders on," David said loudly

"What are you two doing?" Mom asked.

"Ice fishing," David responded with our little secret code to float on the ice down on Sewer Lane. Ever since Whitney's dad killed Peter on the brook and my mother told us not to play on the ice, we started using the code.

"David, let me ask you something," Mom said, folding one of the grocery bags. "Why is it you two always go fishing, but you never take any fishing equipment with you?"

"It's because we leave the gear in the fishing hut on the river's edge," he said, pulling a lie out of his ass.

"Oh," she replied looking at him straight in the eye. "What fishing hut?"

I could tell David struggled a little to come up with a good answer. "The fishing hut down at Wallace's boatyard."

"Oh," My mother said again. She knew he was lying as well as I did but seemed to decide to let it go.

"You ready?" David said looking at me, hoping we could leave quickly. I ran back upstairs to get ready.

David and I walked down the street toward Sewer Lane remembering Peter and how we found him dead. As we turned the corner heading toward the river, we saw Whitney getting into her father's new Mercedes with her mother. She pressed her fingers to her mouth and blew me a kiss with a smile and waved as they backed out of the driveway. "I love that girl," I said.

"I know," David replied and walked down the hill. I stood there in the middle of the road watching the car until it was out of sight, and then caught up with him. We stopped short when we saw dozens of cars parked on River Road up and down both sides. I instantly knew why there were so many cars when I looked at the Cass' house. I could see inside the windows that there were a lot of people moving around. Peter had a lot of family, I guess.

"That prick deserved to die," I said. "I'm so friggin' glad he's dead."

"Look up there in the bedroom window," David said. I looked up and saw Peter's brother, Roger, staring down at us. He gave us the finger and gestured to us he was gonna slice our necks just like his brother's was. I, in turn, flipped him the finger, and yelled "Fuck you!" as loud as I could. The front door swung open, and out came Peter's mom in a raging mood.   "Come over here, you little shits!" she yelled. David and I ran down the street as fast as we could with our waders on. I looked back and saw her waving her arms in the air.

"Get over here, you assholes." We heard her shout again. We ignored her and just kept on running until we got to Sewer Lane.

6

Mr. Brian S. Williams shuffled into the courtroom that was filled with onlookers for his arraignment for the murder of Peter Cass. He wore an orange jump suit, leather belt wrapped around his waist with chains and handcuffs clamped tight to his wrists. He was escorted to the defense area, surrounded by an old wooden railing that moved when you leaned against it with two armed sheriffs on either side of him.

He shifted his eyes around the courtroom. It was full of angry people whispering to each other, pointing and staring at him. He searched for his wife Barbara and saw her sitting on the end of the bench wearing all black. Her eyes stared forward

"All rise for the honorable Judge Susan McCarran." The court bailiff called. Mr. Williams was already standing since the sheriffs were holding each arm. He watched the judge sit down in her chair and put on her glasses, which were hanging around her neck on a colorful chain. She looked sternly at him over the rims, seeming to already to pass judgment because of the charges brought up against him.

"Mr. Brian S. Williams." The judge's voice echoed across the court room. "You are being charged with one count of first degree murder. How do you plead?"

"The bastard is guilty!" A fat man yelled from the back of the courtroom, scaring the people in front of him. The judge slammed her mallet down until the courtroom became silent once again. "Anymore outbursts and you will be removed from the courtroom!" The judge paused for a moment, looking at everyone. Once she was satisfied with her order of the court, she continued with the arraignment.

"Mr. Williams, how do you plead?" she asked again. Silence fell over the courtroom. You could here a pin drop a hundred feet away it was so quiet.

"I'm as guilty as charged your honor. Peter Cass brutally raped my daughter Whitney, so I took the law into my own hands and killed that son of a bitch. The damn police didn't do anything about it, so I did." The courtroom erupted, and the judge began banging her gavel again. Williams turned and looked at his wife, still staring forward as though she was waiting in front of a shop counter, then lunged toward the sheriff on his left, grabbed the gun out of his holster, and fell to the floor holding the gun tight against him. He quickly turned the gun and pointed it toward his chin, resting the barrel on the leather belt. He looked one more time at his wife, then smiled at her before pulling the trigger. The bullet shot threw the bottom of his chin, out the top of his head, striking the ankle of an older security guard.

His wife stared at him with no expression. The sheriff had grabbed the barrel, when he felt the gun go off in his hand trying to pull it away from Mr. Williams. The courtroom was silent for a moment, then again erupted into chaos when the audience saw the blood and dead body of Mr. Williams.

Mrs. Williams turned and left the courtroom, pulling her wedding band off her finger and tossing it into the nearest trashcan as she walked toward the main doors. The police came rushing through the doors within seconds of hearing about the shooting on the police radio and passed her like the wind. She wondered what kind of life she'd have after his funeral while she pushed the main doors open, feeling the cold air rush into her face. She walked down the cement veranda toward a car where her boyfriend sat waiting for her. They'd been involved ever since she'd found out about her husband and Mrs. Clancy.

"Let's go home." She said, slamming the passenger door shut.

"What's going on in there?" Richie asked, starting the car. "Why are all the police showing up?"

"Brian just shot himself in the head," she told him, slipping on her dark sunglasses.

"What? He's dead?"

"Put it this way. I'm not getting any life insurance because of his stupidity," she said, watching the ambulance stopping in front of the main entrance.

"Let's get the hell out of here." Barbara said, waving her hand toward the windshield.

Richie stepped on the gas and drove away as Mrs. Williams closed her eyes, leaning her head back against the headrest. She saw her husband's death over and over in her mind. She wanted to cry. She wanted to care, but her marriage had been shattered. She just didn't care.

"What are you going to do about Whitney?" Richie asked. "How are you going to tell her?"

"That little street rat had to get a goddamn abortion yesterday," she spat. "I'll tell her by letting her read the front page of tomorrow's newspaper. Richie looked at her thinking she was being a little too harsh on her only daughter. "He was her father you know."

"That didn't give him the right to, let's say, do inappropriate things to her when she was younger.

"I can see why you're glad he's dead now."

"Richie you don't even know half of what he's done. The only thing I'm not happy about is, is . . . Forget it, just go home."

"Okay."

7

The judge dropped her glasses off her nose with her mouth open in a state of shock. She looked at the older security guard moaning in pain, holding his ankle. She jumped out of her chair, and ran into her private chambers, putting her hands over her face, feeling like she failed for the first time in her career. "Gain strength," she said out loud, taking a deep lasting breath. "Come on, Susie, relax, it was just another criminal. It was nobody you knew, just relax." She fanned her face with her hands for a moment, and then opened the door to the courtroom.

The police were everywhere, in every corner of the courtroom, the lobby, and around the building.

"Your Honor, are you okay?" a court security officer asked, walking toward her. The judge looked at him wiping the blood and nervous sweat off his hands.

"I'm fine. I just can't believe that man killed himself in front of me." The security officer stood over her like a basketball player, watching the scene being handled in a professional manner.

He slid his hand over his bald head feeling the perspiration. He looked at his partner getting medical attention, and wondered how many weeks he's going to milk the state before he'll return to work   "I think court has adjourned for today, Your Honor," he said, throwing the once white towel in the small canister behind her. The judge looked at him with a small frightened smile.

"Yes, it has, Sam," she agreed

Sam stayed with the judge while the dead Mr. Brian Williams was transported out of the room in a zipped up, bright orange body bag covered with a white sheet.

"So that's it," the judge said, crossing her arms.

"Your Honor, are you okay?" a police officer with a black handlebar mustache asked, walking over to her.

"I'm fine, Officer."

The police officer looked up at Sam and nodded, then turned back to the judge. "The captain wants me to ask you a few questions about the incident, and what you saw."

"What I saw was the son of a bitch shot himself. Everyone else saw the same damn thing. Why don't you go ask the rest of the courtroom, and get the hell out of my chambers!"

8

I heard David stomping up the stairs to my room.

"Jesus, David, loud enough," I said.

"New boots," he replied, and then sat at the top of the steps and leaned against the paneled wall. "Whitney's dad killed himself yesterday."

"What?" I asked.

"He shot himself in the head at the court house," he explained.

"Wow, what the fuck?"

"I don't know, man. My father read the story to me a few minutes ago, and then he told me to stay away from Whitney. She's bad news. Christ, *he's* friggin' bad news."

"Your father can be a real dickhead sometimes," I said.

"Can be? He *is* a dickhead. You don't have to live with him. One of these days I'm outta here. So far outta here, he'll need a plane to come see me."

"So you wanna go and see how she's doing?" I asked, changing the subject before David got pissed off thinking about his own problems.

"Not really. I'd rather go uptown and hang

out in front of Richdale's and see what's going on in town."

"Why?" I said. "There's nothing up there, and I don't have any money." I actually did have some birthday money left in my pocket but hanging out in town seemed stupid and a waste of time to me.

"I don't know. Something to do, I guess."

"Let's go down to Whitney's and see how she's doing, and then we'll go uptown and hang out."

David nodded and got up.

We walked down the stairs where my mother was watching the news. Every time Mr. Willman's name was mentioned, my mother shook her head in disappointment.

"Mom, we're going uptown. We'll be back in a little while," I told her.

"All right," she said, and smiled at us with her famous fake smile.

We passed the bashed in mailboxes on the corner of the street, the result of older teens playing mailbox baseball, and saw two police cruisers parked in front of Whitney's house. We walked down and I expected to see Whitney standing in front of her bedroom window crying. Instead we saw her standing outside in the freezing cold, in her usual spot in the yard doing what she loved to do in the warmer weather, paint.

"Hey!" I yelled as we walked toward her, stomping through the snow. I saw her eyes were puffy with tears, and her nose was running. She was freezing, but she didn't seem to care. She lowered her arms, and dropped the paintbrush and the homemade paint board her father made filled with old dried colors into the snow.

"I heard," I said holding my hands out to give her a consoling hug. She ignored me and stared at the canvas. I walked over anyway and held her tight, when suddenly I could feel her falling apart against me, feeling her fingers pushing against the thickness of my coat, and sinking her head deep into my shoulder.

"My mother threw the newspaper at me and told me to read about my son-of-a-bitch father," she said, wiping her tears with the sleeve of her paint-splattered, gray sweatshirt she wore every time she got the urge to paint.

I looked at David standing near the canvas, shivering with cold, looking down at his new boots. I squeezed Whitney with affection, holding her as long and as much as she wanted me to. I didn't care what David was thinking, and I didn't even care if he just left. I was here for her, and that's all I cared about.

"Whitney!" Her mother screamed out the back door startling her and me. Whitney jumped away from me and quickly held onto her stomach like she was ready to vomit.

"Come down later. I have to go," she said, walking away at a snail's pace and slightly crouched over. I looked down and saw the paintbrush and board, thinking about when and where the funeral was going to be, and would I be allowed to go out of respect for Whitney-my girl.

"Let's go," David said, picking up the paint board and brush, and placing them on the stool next to the tripod. I wondered why Whitney was trying to paint outside in the freezing cold when she had a place down in the basement that her father made for her three years ago. I touched the canvas to see if the paint was dry. It was frozen. When I actually looked at the canvas filled with odd shaded colors, I noticed she was painting a picture of herself standing in the middle of a tall grass field with nothing around as far as the eye could see. I began to realize what she was painting. I saw her thoughts permanently written on canvas. She was alone. I watched Whitney slowly step into the house, still holding her stomach.

"Let's go," David said again, putting his hand on the back of my shoulder.

We finally made it uptown after walking through the harsh wind of the open highway. My face felt chapped and raw with cold. I wanted to go home and stay inside. I wanted to hold Whitney. I wanted to do something other than walk uptown but satisfying David's little, I-want-to-go-hang-out-fix was what I needed to do since he stood like a bump on a log at Whitney's for almost a good half hour in silence. I figured I owed it to him.

Suddenly, a red beat up Chevy Silverado pickup truck, came squealing around the corner and slid to a stop right in front of us. It was

Jonathan Felder, the only black kid in the town of Merrimac. He had his two sexy looking girl-friends, Dottie and Deanna Brown—Tweedle Dotz and Tweedle Ditz we called them. They were two of the most brainless girls on the face of the earth, and they lived in town just before the Amesbury line. Jonathan always had them with him and we all knew why.

"Hey," Jonathan said, slamming the truck into park. I could hear the girls giggling. Jonathan pulled a cigarette from behind his ear. "You want to buy some shit today?" he asked, lighting his cigarette with one quick flick of his Zippo lighter. David glanced at me, then stared hard at Jonathan. "No, not today," he said clenching his fists, and then he put his hands in his coat pockets.

One of the girls turned around and bent over the seat of the truck to reach for something and stuck her ass in the air.

"Bitch, will you sit down!" Jonathan shouted shaking his head. "I got to go," he said, slamming the truck into gear, and spun the tires when he drove off.

I gave David a dirty look as we walked to the nearest store to get out of the cold for a few minutes.

"Let's go home." David said before I got to the door.

"Let's get something to drink first." I said pulling out a five-dollar bill. David's eyes lit up like I hit the jackpot.

"My treat," I said looking into his eyes holding back a smile. I knew what he was thinking about, but I also knew he wasn't going to ask me either. Thank God.

David and I walked in my house and found my mother had fallen asleep in front of the television. We walked upstairs and tossed our boots off and threw the coats on the spare bed in my room. When I lay down on my bed and thought about Whitney, I wondered how she was doing. I was glad Peter Cass was dead. One less disgusting skinner the world has to deal with. I was glad Mr. Williams had taken him out. But the whole thing was still sad and complicated. I turned to David. "Hey, turn on the TV, will ya?"

9

Whitney's mother picked up the phone just after four thirty in the morning, and heard a man's deep voice on the other side.

"Barbara?" the voice questioned.

"Yes?" she answered. "Richie is that you?" she asked.

"Yes. I have some bad news. It's your mother. Her house is on fire."

"Oh God, is she all right?" she asked, jumping out of bed, and turned on the light. She quickly opened the dresser drawer and pulled out her gray sweatshirt and pants.

"Your mother was transported to the Anna Jacques Hospital. I'll explain more when you get here."

"Richie, is she hurt?" she asked again. The phone went dead silent. She waited for Richie to answer.

"Richie, is Mom okay?" she asked again starting to panic. Unexpectedly she heard a click with a loud annoying dial tone that followed.

She slammed the phone down in anger and raced around her bedroom trying to get dressed as fast as she could. She ran down the stairs to the living room where she kept the car keys. She heard Whitney calling her from the top of the stairs half asleep.

"Whit, go back to bed. I have to go somewhere; I'll be back soon." She said, opening the front door and putting her coat on. She ran to the car. The sub-zero temperature sent chills through her body.

She jumped into her husband's new Mercedes and backed out of the driveway. She slammed on the brakes when she saw a police cruiser stop directly behind her. She hit the horn in anger, yelling at whoever was inside the car, when unexpectedly she heard a voice next to the driver's window. She looked through the window and saw a policeman standing inches away and then quickly rolled down the window.

"Officer Mathias, I don't have time to talk to you about my husband; he's dead." She shouted. "I need to go to the hospital!"

"Mrs. Williams, please shut off the car and step out."

"Mark, you don't understand. I need to get to the hospital." She shouted in hysterics. "My mother is there. Something has happened to her!"

The officer opened the door of the car and reached in and shut off the engine. "Please step out of the car, Mrs. Williams." He said again.

"I don't understand. What the hell is going on here?" She snapped. "My mother's house is on fire. She was brought to the hospital and all you want to do is ask me the same damn questions about my husband that you've asked me a hundred times already! Now let me go!"

"Barbara, I'm here because of your mother. Now, let's go inside where it's warm, so we can talk about it." Barbara instantly realized something else has happened to her mother other than just going to the hospital.

"My mother . . . she's dead, isn't she, Mark?" she calmly asked, crossing her arms.

"Barbara, let's go inside." Barbara led the way when Whitney flicked on the outside light and opened the door.

"Mom?" she said, instantly recognizing Officer Mark Mathias behind her.

"Mark? What are you doing here?"

"Whitney, go back to bed. Mark is here to talk to me about something."

"Honey, I'm sorry about your father." He said giving her a slight hug. "I think you should stay and listen to what I have to say, because this concerns you too." He watched Barbara taking off her coat, as he tried to think of an easy way to break the news. "Barbara, you and Whitney need to sit down." He said waving his hand toward the living room.

Whitney slowly walked to the couch holding her stomach and carefully sat down putting her feet on the cushions. Her mother stood near the coffee table with her arms crossed, pacing and refusing to sit down. Mark took a deep breath and stared into her eyes.

"Barbara. Your mother didn't make it out of the house." He said in a low tone waiting for her to lose control. Whitney spun around quickly and shouted. "What, what happened to grandma?" "Barbara, Whitney, I'm sorry." Mark said quietly. "If you want, I can take you to the hospital. Richie is there. He's waiting for you." Barbara quickly turned her head and looked at him wondering how he knew about her and Richie. She nodded her head, accepting his offer and went to put her coat back on wondering what kind of condition her mother will be in from the fire

10

Officer Mathias pulled up to the hospital's emergency entrance. Before the car stopped, Barbara jumped out when she saw Richie standing in the lobby, still in his firefighter's uniform, holding his helmet. She ran into the lobby and wrapped her arms around him. This time she didn't care anymore about keeping her relationship with Richie a secret; she really didn't have any reason to. Richie held her tight as the tears poured from her eyes. He shook hands with Mark, and lightly nudged Barbara toward the elevator.

"Your mother is downstairs in the morgue, Barbara." Richie said

Richie slowly opened the door to the morgue, and led Barbara in. The overhead lights were lightly shadowed from curtain dividers hanging from the ceiling. The air felt cold and stale. The room was avocado-green and filled with small, stainless steel doors along the left wall, like a little dormitory room with refrigerators.

Mark and Richie stood close to Barbara as the forensic pathologist opened the steel door where her mother lay and slid her out on a long stainless steel table.

"Wait," she said, closing her eyes tight. She wanted to gain strength before she saw the horror that awaited her. She took a long nervous breath and released it slowly. "Okay," she said, opening her eyes. She watched the doctor carefully slip the white sheet down and uncovered her mother just enough to expose her face. The only part of her face that was burned was the right side of her cheek. Barbara was relieved she wasn't badly burned until the doctor pulled the sheet down further to her waist and revealed the rest of her mother. The mid-portion of her mother was burned all the way through, the size of a basketball. She quickly grabbed Richie by the arm to hold herself from fainting. "How did the fire start in her house?" she asked Richie.

"From my experience," the doctor spoke loudly slurring his words. "I don't think anything in your mother's house had anything to do with the fire. It looks to be the fire started in your mother's abdominal area."

"What?" Barbara asked, confused, looking at Richie. "That's impossible."

"No, it is possible. It's called SHC. Human spontaneous combustion, is when a body has a chemical imbalance in the stomach, or intestinal area, which has created too much methane gas. It ignites like a match that causes an extremely quick fire. Most of the time, the body will burn from the inside out, thus quickly reducing the body to ashes. But in your mother's case, and the age she was, it's possible her body ignited and set the house on fire. But it's not impossible to have happened. It is rare. When the fire started, she could have been near a window and ignited the curtains or something else that could have quickly caught fire."

"I don't believe this. What kind of a doctor are you?"

"Thank you, Doctor," Mark said, grasping Barbara's arm and pulling her toward the door.

They stepped off the elevator back in to the emergency area. Barbara walked toward the door in a hurry, and then stopped before they automatically opened. She turned around and looked at Mark and Richie. "Which one of you two is giving me a ride home?" she asked, holding back the tears.

"I will," Richie said, putting his hands in his pockets.

"Will you stay?" she asked.

Richie looked at her and hesitated. "Let's get you home. I'll stay."

11

Saturday morning, Whitney opened another bottle of Ibuprofen from the medicine cabinet after eating the first one like wintergreen Lifesavers. She kept telling her mother they made her feel better. Maybe it helped her cope with the loss of her father and her grandmother within days from each other. Her English teacher called yesterday concerned, asking when Whitney was returning to school. "Give her time. She was fuckin raped, remember!" She then rudely slammed down the phone, quickly cutting off the conversation. "Jesus Christ, have a little respect!" she shouted walking into the kitchen.

Whitney shut the medicine cabinet and looked at herself in the mirror. She didn't like what she saw. She realized she hadn't taken a hot shower since she came home from "the killing clinic," as she referred to it. She told herself when she turned sixteen, if she ever got pregnant by accident, she was going to have the baby, but since this pregnancy was no accident, or by choice, she didn't oppose the abortion. In her mind, she wanted to kill Peter.

She shut the bathroom door and took off her T-shirt. She pulled down her sweat pants leaving her red skimpy little underwear on and turned on the hot water. She looked at herself again before the steam fogged up the mirror and looked at her breasts. She wondered what she would look like with bigger ones, like some of the Hollywood actresses and would she be just as attractive, if not better. She swiped her hand across the steamed up mirror, slid out of her underwear, and jumped into the hot shower.

I left my house before David would call or come down, whichever came first and walked down to Whitney's house. I knocked on the door, hearing the usual echoing through the old hallway inside. Whitney's mother opened it and looked at me as though I was a Cass. But she spoke almost politely to me, which was a surprise. "Come in. She's upstairs in her room." She went back to whatever she was doing and left me to shut the door. I walked up the twenty-six steps of stairs to the second floor and walked down the long hallway toward Whitney's room. I always felt I needed a map to find my way around Whitney's house. When she and I were young kids we played hide and seek, because it was so full of cool places to hide. When I was "it," Whitney would always let me stay hiding for a long time and then laugh when I came out looking for her.

I knocked on her open bedroom door,

whispering her name. I walked in looking at all the bright white walls with pictures of successful teenage stars. I sat on her little, white dresser chair next to the window over looking the street and waited until she came back. Unexpectedly, I saw her walk in and shut the door. She was wearing nothing but a faded pink towel wrapped around her wet body with a blue towel around her head. I realized she didn't even know I was in the room when she dropped the towel and threw it on the bed baring her beautiful naked body. I looked at her with total admiration. She was so beautiful, soft to the eyes. Her body was smooth, slim, and full of sexy curves just like the models in a magazine. Her breasts were as perfect as I've always imagined, and her legs were... wow.

I didn't want to say anything, but I knew she would soon discover me sitting there, and possibly be frightened.

"Hey," I said softly. She put her foot up on the bed sliding her hands up and down her leg with lotion as though she didn't hear me. "Hey," I said louder. Whitney turned her head toward me and smiled. "I already knew you were in here," she said and stood up facing me, giving me the complete frontal view of her.

"Do you think I'm pretty?"

I stood up feeling my arousal rubbing against my pants, looking at her from head to toe. I wanted her forever. I wanted to hold her beautiful smooth body against me. What I wanted was a miracle.

"Do you think I'm pretty?" she asked again.

"Whitney," I said nervously, trembling inside. "There's nobody on the face of this earth that's more beautiful than you. You're the most beautiful girl I've ever seen, and you'll always be the most beautiful girl, ever."

She took the towel off her head, letting her wet hair drop around her shoulders, covering parts of her breasts, and put her hand against her side like she was posing for me.

"Look at me," she said, putting her right foot forward. "What do you want to do with me?" she asked. I thought she was kidding around until I looked into her eyes and realized the question is not what I wanted; it's what she wanted. I smiled as wide as I could, wanting to go crazy. My hormones were raging; I wanted her in every way possible.

I walked closer to her, shaking, and scared of what I was about to do. I had dreamed about this moment with her as long as I could remember, and now the dream was about to come true.

I put my hands around her waist feeling the wetness of her shower, and kissed her ever so lightly on the lips. I could feel her tremble. We kissed, letting our tongues touch for the first time. That day I didn't have the slightest clue of what I was doing, but I let all the wonderful thoughts and the heat of the moment take its course.

I walked home after we made love, thinking about her in a totally new way. Thinking of her soft body close to mine, her passionate kiss still tingled on my lips, the smell of her shampoo in her long hair. She was no longer just my friend. I had truly fallen in love with her. And, even though it was only three degrees outside, I was sweating.

12

Barbara drove into the gravel driveway of her mother's partially burned Cape home with light blue shutters surrounded by a row of rose bushes. She parked in front of the garage as she did every time she came over, only this time, everything seemed different to her.

She slowly put the car in park, looking at the old house. She saw the charred upper side of the house where the fire broke out, where her mother died. The window overlooking the garage was smashed and burned all the way through. Barbara saw the yellow caution tape surrounding the house and opened the car door. She instantly smelled the burned wood, as though someone had a wood-stove going. It smelled good, almost relaxing. But the breadth of what had happened hit her full force. "Now what the hell am I going to do?" she said.

She walked slowly toward the front door looking at the rest of the house. She angrily ripped the yellow tape from across the door and threw it aside, and then took a deep breath when she touched the door handle to the screen door. She closed her eyes for a moment, opened the door and stepped into the breezeway. She immediately stumbled over the clutter spread throughout the breezeway. There were assorted house plants, pictures, even an old Cuckoo clock from Germany, which Barbara's grandmother had brought to the U.S. in 1881. She looked around as though it was her first time she had ever been inside, feeling like a stranger, although this was where she grew up.

She could smell the extinguished fire still lingering in the air as she walked around looking at the walls. She still couldn't get it through her head that her mother was dead. She stepped up into the kitchen as though she stepped into the fifties. The tiles on the floor were black and white. The table was oval shaped against the wall, with a steel border around the tabletop. A rug lay underneath where her dad's dogs always slept. Her mom never removed the rug, in remembrance of her dad, and of the dogs Snoopy, and Spotty. The black Labrador Retrievers were their other children. She looked at the huge refrigerator and opened it up wondering if she still had Dad's same old beer on the door from when he died in 1961. She did. "Mom, you never did change, did you?

Barbara walked up the hardwood stairs off of the parlor, just after the twin Lazy Boy recliners and looked at her mother's bedroom door. It was closed. The fireman must have closed it hoping that maybe the fire wouldn't spread through the whole house. She touched the door handle quickly expecting it to still be hot. It wasn't. She opened the door and saw the charred wall with a big hole from where the water came through trying to douse the flames. Her eyes flooded with tears when she looked down at the floor and saw her mothers favorite Bible. She picked it up, held it tight to her chest, and knelt down on the floor. She cried, dropping her head down to her chest. "What am I gonna do now?" She cried. "Why did you leave me now? I need you!"

She forced herself to regain control and placed the Bible on the bed. She got up off her knees and carefully slid her hand across her mother's bureau. She walked out of the room hoping she would wake up from this awful nightmare, but she knew it was all too real and too devastating, and she knew she would have to face the facts sometime soon.

When she opened the bedroom door to her old room and walked in, she thought she heard her name being called. Then, she heard it again. A chill went through her. "Barbara?" She heard it again, but it wasn't her mother's voice. She turned around and saw Richie standing in the doorway. "This was your old room?" he asked quietly. "Very sweet" He gestured at the walls, painted a soft shade of pink, the ballet slippers hanging near the window next to her dress, and all the white furniture around the room.

"Yeah, I loved my room," Barbara said. "Mom left everything the same when I went to college.

She wanted me to come back home when I graduated, but I ended up quitting school and getting married to that . . . to Brian. I was pregnant. "Now look at the shit I'm in. Brian's dead because of that slut of a daughter I have. I'm in a rotten mess. Moms gone now, no money left, and payments due."

"I'm sorry about your mom," Richie told her. "And I can help you with the house, and lend you some money."

"No, Richie I don't want your money, but I would like your help cleaning out the house. But what am I going to do with all this stuff? I know some of it can come home with me but the big stuff? I don't know. Maybe I'll just toss everything. It's ruined anyway."

"Why don't you get your mother's funeral arrangements taken care of first, and then worry about the house later."

"How did you know I was here anyway?" she asked

"The neighbor next door called the police, and Mark called me. Barbara, you're not supposed to be in here. It's dangerous.

"Dangerous? It's not dangerous in here, and besides, it's my house now, so you can tell that old train wreck of a woman next door to mind her damn business."

"Okay, Barbara, I'm not going to argue with you. I'm just letting you know you're not supposed to be here. Call me when you get home."

"Richie," she said and looked deep into his eyes. "I, I'm…" Barbara wanted to apologize for being snappy, but she couldn't say the words. "I'm ready to go home now. I don't want to be here anymore, not just yet, anyway."

"Barbara, someday, you're going to have to face your demons."

"No, I want to go home now. I can't do this." She walked down the steps and swung open the front door. She flipped the next door neighbor the finger and jumped into her car. She put the car in reverse, and then slammed on the brake, almost backing into Richie's truck. "Richie!" she shouted. Richie came out of the house. "Move your damn truck!" Richie nodded and put his hands up, as if telling her to stop. He backed the truck out of her way, and she swerved, again nearly hitting him as she backed out of the driveway and took off down the road.

"I never should've married that asshole," she said to herself. "I never should've had kids. I should've just listened to Dad before he died, and just stayed home."

13

Two weeks passed by after my wonderful day with Whitney with no sign of her. I walked down the street on a freezing cold Sunday morning, my face feeling ready to crack like the thick ice covering Sewer Lane. I saw Whitney's mother getting out of a big pickup truck with a big firefighter's sticker on the back window, laughing as though everything in her life was just perfect. I watched her for a moment, falling all over some man I had never seen before. The man wrapped his arms around her, lifted her up, and carried her to the door laughing and slipping on the ice

I squished a small snowball in my hand and threw it up to Whitney's window, hoping and praying she would come to the window with that beautiful smile of hers. I threw another snowball, but this time it was solid and bigger, splattering it hard against the house.

"Whitney's not here, so stop throwing snowballs at my house, you little shit," I heard her mother say as she leaned against the house lighting a cigarette

"Is she coming back soon?" I asked, hearing

her giggle when her friend slid his hands under her coat. "I said is she coming back soon?" I shouted as though I was the boss of the neighborhood. Her mother stopped giggling, pushed her friend's hands away, and walked over to me, flicking the half-burned cigarette into the snow. She stopped in front of me, staring at me like she wanted to stuff my head into the ground. I could smell the raw odor of hard liquor seeping from her.

"You're drunk," I said as she tipped to one side, catching herself before she fell to the ground.

"Who the hell do you think you are?" She said in a low tone of voice. I looked at her friend standing there holding himself up against the house, hoping he wouldn't come over and punch me out for being snappy at his so-called date. Whitney's mother leaned closer to me, breathing her stench against my face, staring hard into my eyes. I was a little afraid she was going to hit me.

"If you'd been through what I've been through, you little twerp, you'd be getting drunk too!"

When she raised her arm, I flinched thinking she was going to smack me in the face, but she turned around and stumbled to the front door, and began to giggle again as though I was never there. I looked up at Whitney's window and saw the curtain move. She was home, and she knew I saw her. I kept my eyes glued to her window and started to slowly walk back up the hill. I smiled when I saw her hand press against the window as if she was saying hi. I stared up at her window the whole time, hoping she'd ask me to come in and keep her company. She never did. Then to my surprise, I heard someone yelling.

14

"How did it feel?" I heard someone say again. I looked around wondering where the voice was coming from, and then there she was, Meredith, aka Cheater, Chandler sticking her face out her bedroom window.

"What are you doing?" she shouted. Whitney's dog was barking again.

"Nothing, going home," I said. "How did what feel?"

Meredith was somewhat of a cute girl with blonde hair, blue eyes, and big boobs. She was French Canadian. We nicknamed her Cheater, because she always cheated on her boyfriends. And she has had boyfriends from a really early age, maybe because her boobs grew faster than the rest of her, or maybe because it was rumored that her uncle Richard stayed over the summer she turned eleven, and had a quiet date one night in her room when everyone else was sleeping. But for some unknown reason she's always wanted to, as she called it, "tag" David. Sometimes I wish David would just give in and do her, and get it over with, but he always mentioned the disease no one else dared to say: V.D. But I actually believed he was a little scared to lose his virginity. I know I was.

"Whitney! How was it?" she asked. I barely heard her from that damn dog barking loud enough to drown out a jackhammer. I wished again that someone would shoot that dog so the whole neighborhood could get some friggin' peace.

"What are you talking about?" I asked her, knowing exactly what she was talking about.

"Don't play stupid with me. You tagged Whitney. She called and told me all about it," she shouted loud enough so my mother could've heard her, and then raised the window a little higher. "She said you were great!" she yelled again. My face felt like it could melt the snow it was so red. I was stuck in the middle of lying, and running. Suddenly, Cheater and I looked at each other in shock when we heard a loud popping sound coming from Whitney's house, like someone was shot. And then there was another. We both knew what that noise was.

15

"Stay there. I'm coming out," Cheater said and slammed the window. I realized the dog wasn't barking anymore and stared down the street at Whitney's house. Meredith came running out in her ugly pair of dark green sweat pants and her usual wife beater tank top showing skin, a lot of it. She tried covering her protruding nipples with her arms from the cold, and then quickly ran back to the house for her coat.

"What do you think that noise was?" she asked, zipping up her coat and slipping her hands inside the front of her sweat pants

"I know what that noise was. I just hope nobody is dead over there," I said.. Anyway, It's really none of our business. I'm sure we'll find out sooner or later.

"Think we should go down and see?" she asked.

For that one little instant she said those words, I pictured Whitney dead on her bedroom floor with a bullet embedded into her skull, and her drunken mother standing over her holding the smoking gun.

Cheater and I slowly walked down the road looking at Whitney's house, wondering what, and who, when suddenly we saw her mother's friend stumbling out of the house holding onto his left arm. He jumped into his truck and backed out of the driveway in a hurry, spinning the tires down the road. We heard sirens in the distance.

"What the hell's going on over there?" Cheater wrapped her arms around my arm, and tightened up with fear.

"We have to go see if Whitney's okay," she said, squeezing my arm a little harder. I didn't know whether she was holding my arm for a sense of protection or was it that she was holding my arm with affection? It felt great, and she smelled good with that perfume she likes to wear all the time.

We walked down to Whitney's house and stared at the front door from the run down porch.

Awfully quiet, I thought, raising my hand to knock on the door. Cheater quickly knocked before I did and stuck her hand under my arm again. The door slowly opened. Whitney stood there with her little doggie pajama bottoms and matching pajama top unbuttoned low enough to reveal the sides of her breasts. Cheater let go of my arm and walked in the house breathing a sigh of relief and gave her a big hug. She quickly looked around, and I followed her in. We found Whitney's mother passed out on the couch wearing a black lace bra. She had a shirt tucked under her head for a pillow.

Whitney looked at me and held up her arms as she started to cry. I took her in my arms and held her. Whitney reached out and shut the door still holding me tight and kissed me on the neck.

"Are you okay?" I asked squeezing her tighter. I wanted to bring her upstairs and hold her like before, but the thought quickly left my mind when Cheater came back into the living room holding a handgun.

"Cheater, that's my mom's," Whitney said, holding her hand out to retrieve it from her but still holding me with her other arm.

Cheater raised it up toward the ceiling aiming at the light.

"What's it doing on the kitchen counter, Whit?"

Whitney looked at me as she buttoned the rest of her pajama top and took a deep breath. You could tell she was looking for a way out of that question, but she didn't have the slightest clue of how to answer it. She held her hand out again looking at Cheater still holding the gun like she was going to shoot something.

"Cheater, let me have the gun!" She shouted louder. I got the impression something else was wrong because Whitney seemed awfully cold and raw toward Meredith.

"What's the gun for, Whit?"

"Maybe her mother was keeping it there for her own protection, Cheater. Who knows?" I said sarcastically, hoping Cheater would just drop the questions.

Cheater looked at Whitney's mom still passed out on the couch.

"What were the loud noises we heard, Whit?" she asked, still looking around for anything out of the ordinary.

"What are you, a cop?" Whitney shouted loud enough that her mother moved around on the couch.

"Whitney, we thought someone got shot, and then we saw your mom's friend running out of the house." Whitney knew what she was talking about, but she was unwilling to tell her the truth. "I-I-I don't know what you mean?"

I unzipped my coat and stood there feeling the warmth from the heater vent I was standing on. Cheater stood next to the couch looking at me, gesturing me to get her to tell the truth.

"Cheater, maybe the noise we heard wasn't from here. Maybe we just thought it came from here. Let's just forget it," I said, trying to make everything better.

"Maybe you're right. I just thought ..."

"You just thought what?" Whitney snapped. Cheater looked at Whitney with her eyes staring hard.

"Nothing, I'm sorry, Whit." She said, walking over to give her another hug. Whitney turned her head and walked away from her.

"Meredith," she said in a low whisper. "I want you to leave."

Cheater nodded at her, then zipped up her coat to her chin. She looked at me like she was ready to cry and grabbed my arm, pulling me close.

"Not this time, Cheater, he stays with me," Whitney said, loud and clear. Cheater dropped her arms from me and opened the door. She walked out without looking back and slammed the door. I looked at Whitney wondering why she was being so cruel to her best friend, and then I saw Whitney unbuttoning her pajama top with a smile on her face like nothing ever happened. She looked at her mother and lightly took my hand and led me up the stairs to her room.

"Things are different with us. You're with me now, and we'll always be together, forever." I didn't know what she meant by that but following her to her room, smelling her unforgettable perfume, and with what I knew was going to be next, I didn't care.

After we'd, well, tagged. I slid off the bed and looked out her bedroom window at the yard and pool below, thinking how lucky I was to finally have the girl I'd been crazy about for all these years, when I saw the family dog, lying next to his doghouse in a frozen puddle of blood. I looked back at Whitney, but she was in bed, sleeping with a strange smile on her face.

16

My mother dropped me off at the store after a dreadful morning at the dentist, so I could get some jaw breakers. I saw David and his druggie friend Luke still watching Tweedle Ditz showing off her favorite asset and shouted just as a loud Mack truck was passing through the square. When the truck passed, David saw me looking and quickly handed the bag to Luke. I waved at him acting like I didn't see what he just did and went into the store pissed off. I stood there in the store looking out the window with the overhead heater blowing directly on me, staring at David and Luke and began to wonder if my best friend was turning into one of those druggies.

I paid for my candy still staring out the window and headed for the door, when I saw Jonathan's beat up truck pulling up in front of the store blocking my view of David. "Shit," I said softly walking out of the store still watching surreptitiously. Jonathan spotted me, looked at me with his beady black eyes, pretty much telling me to piss off. He drove off, spinning his tires. Jonathan and I never got along ever since we went to the so-called summer camp in Amesbury when we were twelve years old. He accused me of sticking a snake in his bed when he was trying to sleep. I should have, or did I? I just don't remember.

What really broke the ice between us is during the summer three years ago, when everyone in the neighborhood went fishing down on Wallace's boatyard. Jonathan said something mean about my sister having one leg shorter than the other, and I came back with, his mother should stick with her own shade of color. We never saw eye to eye after that, and now, well, it didn't matter

David stood on the curb in front of the store standing somewhat away from Luke, watching every move I made, as though I was the bad guy. I just shook my head and started walking home. Then I heard David's whistle echoing through the Merrimac square. I turned around and saw him running toward me holding the bag. Tweedle Ditz surprisingly enough, was running behind David like she was his girl and caught up with him grabbing him by the back of his coat. She pulled against him to stop him from running, kissed him hard on the lips, and walked away smiling.

"What was that for?" I shouted to her.

"I like him!" she shouted back. I couldn't help but laugh. Everyone knew she was Jonathan's little bitch, and no one was allowed to even look at her, much less to touch her or there would be severe consequences.

"It's obvious she wants you, David," I said

with disappointment in my voice.

"No shit, but why?" he asked, when suddenly she came running back.

"Can I walk with you?" she asked, putting her arm around him. David looked at me again. But then she said the magic words: "Jonathan and I are totally over."

"What happened to you and Jonathan?" I asked, as if I really cared, or even believed her. I knew it was a crock of shit. I also knew that, even though she had the body of Miss Massachusetts, she was dumb as dirt.

"He likes to slap Dorothy and me," she replied. "But Dottie is too afraid to tell him off."

I wondered if she was telling the truth, since I'd never seen a bruise on her, unless she knew how to hide them well.

"It's friggin' cold out here," I said as the wind off the open highway blew in our faces, sending goose bumps all over my body. Tweedle Ditz grabbed David's arm, squeezing it tighter. I got tired of sucking on the jawbreaker and spit it over the bridge, watching it until it smashed against the pavement below, and then wiped my chapped lips with my glove, feeling the stick of the candy. David looked at me and with a smile gestured for me to look at Ditz's coat. It's then I noticed that underneath her shiny, bright green coat, she was totally naked. No wonder she was cold. I stopped in front of David and looked down at Ditz's zipper, getting ready to pull it down and confirm she had nothing on underneath.

"What?" she asked, seeing my eyes looking down at her chest, smiling from ear to ear, and reaching for the zipper. "No, I don't have anything on underneath," she said, and started teasingly pulling the zipper down ever so slowly. "I left my shirt at Jonathan's because we got into a fight. He threw my coat at me and then kicked me out of the house. He told me if I want to hang around with him, I'd better start doing what I'm told. That's when he threw the bag at me, and told me to give it to you. By the way, where is the bag?"

"Luke has the bag," David said, looking at me with an, "Oh shit, I've been caught" look on his face.

"Great, Jonathan's not going to like this," She replied still sliding her zipper up and down, until she caught me staring at her again, waiting for her to slide it down a little further. She smiled at me and quickly slid it down to the end, spread her coat apart enough to flash me, and then zipped it up as fast as she could.

"Satisfied?" she asked. I looked at her and paused for a moment.

"No," I said with a smile.

Suddenly we heard the loud exhaust rumble of Jonathan's truck coming up the road. We all thought about jumping the railing and hiding in the snow, but we knew he would see us.

Just as we saw his truck, Jonathan locked up the front tires, and slid the truck down the road until it came to a halt just feet from where we were standing. Tweedle Dotz rolled down the window looking at us with tears running down her face. "Where's the bag, Ditz!" Jonathan shouted.

"Luke has it!" I shouted back and ripped open the passenger door, yanking Dotz out by the front of her purple coat before she could react.

"What the fuck are you doing?" Jonathan shouted louder. I saw his hand grab the handle of his door. I thought for sure we were going to get into a fight and roll around in the snow and ice, but Jonathan knew I wasn't going to back down like everyone else he's had a tiff with because we had one thing in common. We were both wrestlers in school, and every time we were partners, I never lost. He knew I was stronger than him, at least so I thought.

"Put her back in the truck, asshole, or we're gonna go a round!" he shouted.

"Get out of the truck," I said softly, glaring at him. He opened his door still sitting in the truck, staring at me with his beady, black eyes. My body began trembling inside, shaking as if we were standing in the middle of the Antarctic; but at that point of time, I wasn't cold or even thinking about it. My adrenaline was so high, I felt unstoppable.

"You're the asshole everyone talks about, Jonathan!" I shouted. "You're the asshole who hits girls!" Jonathan slammed his door shut and banged the truck into drive still with that hated look on his face. He kept his foot on the brake and stepped on the gas spinning the tires until the back of the truck became nothing but a cloud of smoke.

"Whitney's nothing but a whore!" he shouted, taking his foot off the brake and drove down the road with the tires still spinning into a cloud like the whole street was on fire. We watched him until he was out of sight, smelling the disgusting smell of burnt rubber.

"He's such an asshole!" I shouted.

Tweedle Dotz looked at me with a soft smile and placed her hand on mine. She nodded her head as to say thank you. She never said the words, but I know deep down, she said it in her own way. Ditz reached out and hugged her tight.

"He's got your number," David said. "It's not over yet." I looked back at the blue smoke thinning into the air, thinking of what kind of shit Jonathan was going to pull in the near future. The bad thing about the whole mess is, his cousin is John Wayland, (a.k.a. the leg breaker)

"David," I said softly. "You need to get rid of that bag before you get caught by the cops." He looked at me, pressing against his coat.

"I don't want to," He said. Deanna and Dottie looked at me and knew I meant business. Dottie slid her hand inside David's coat and slowly pulled the bag out and handed it to Deanna

"Ditz, give me the bag," David said. Deanna opened the bag and tossed it high over the railing and down the hill. Everyone watched as the pot scattered all over the snow. No one said anything for a long time. We just watched until it all disappeared into the snow.

"There's going to be a lot of plants coming up in the spring," Ditz said, laughing.

"Great, what about Jonathan's cut?" David asked. "Luke's gonna tell him I have the bag, and he's going to come after me, or his cousin will anyway."

"I'll take care of it," Dottie said. She had a way with Jonathan, and we all knew what she did.

"It's cold out here, let's go home." Ditz said, pulling David by the hand hoping he'd forget about the bag.

"Yeah, David, let's go home," I said.

17

I knocked on the door of Whitney's house thinking about what happened yesterday with Jonathan. I remembered Jonathan calling Whitney a whore. Then defending her reputation in my thoughts, telling myself she couldn't be a whore if the only person she's ever been with, other than the rapist, was me.

Whitney's mother opened the door. She was crying, her mascara running down her face. "She's downstairs," she said, walking away, wiping her eyes. I didn't care what her mother was doing, but I did wonder why she was crying.

As I walked down the steep flight of stairs to her basement, I could smell the strong odor of fresh paint. "Hey," I said, stepping off the last step and into a small puddle of water.

"Watch your step," Whitney said. "It's slippery." I expected to see amateur designs on canvas; instead, I saw something beautiful. Whitney's painting was of a large fifteenth-century wooden ship drifting into an August sunset with a young girl holding onto the wheel.

"Wow!" I said.

"Yeah, this one is my favorite," she said.

I knew this was another about being alone, but this one was so special that I felt sure it should be hanging in an art gallery, and not in some smelly, dark basement. I remembered that my friend, Derek's stepfather was an artist: John Richard Parry. I wondered if perhaps he could help Whitney...

"I want to die like my father did," Whitney said suddenly.

I was in shock. I was mad. I was raging inside.

"I want you to help me die." I clenched my fists, and then I opened my hand and slapped her in the face as hard as I could. She spun around like a top and dropped her brush and homemade paint holder, as she fell hard to the floor. I looked at her, steaming with anger. I was so mad I couldn't speak. I just watched her put her hand on her cheek. She started to cry as she looked at me through the strands of her hair.

"You need fuckin' help," I said in a low tone. I didn't say anything else. I left thinking that was the last time I'd ever see her again. As I walked up the stairs, I heard her say, "I love you," from the bottom of the steps. I stopped at the top and stood there looking at her painting she made for her mother when she was in grade school hanging near the doorway. I didn't look back at her, I couldn't. I just closed the basement door and walked away.

I walked up the hill toward home, crouched down inside my coat trying to keep warm, feeling the rain drops soaking my hair with tears stinging my eyes. I thought about the day I would have to see her in a casket with a bullet hole in her head. Then I heard her yelling. I turned and saw Whitney running up the hill trying to zip up her coat. At the same time, I saw Cheater standing in her bedroom window. She waved at me. I didn't wave back since my hands were glued to the insides of my pockets from the shivering cold. Whitney grabbed my arm and pulled me close to her.

"I'm sorry," she whispered and put her hand on my face. She smiled at me. "Come back. I don't want you to leave. Not today." I glanced at Cheater still standing in her window and then looked at Whitney with her red cheek where I slapped her. I felt guilty. I felt ashamed of myself for doing such a . . . such a Jonathan thing. I pulled my hands out of my pockets and lightly touched her on the other cheek, kissing her on the lips.

"Whitney," I whispered, "You're the reason love even exists."

"Don't leave me," she said. "Come back with me." The rain started coming down harder as we looked into each other's eyes. I didn't care how hard it rained or how cold I was.

"I don't want you to die," I told her. When I said that, she just smiled. Her look seemed almost aloof, like she didn't really care what I wanted. It scared me. It frightened me. We walked back to her house and went back downstairs to the basement.

I watched her finish painting her picture in silence, watching every stroke she made with the different colors. Occasionally she would turn around and smile at me, and every so often she would unbutton one of her buttons on her ugly pajama top. After the last button she teasingly unbuttoned, I walked behind her and wrapped my arms around her body feeling the warmth of her soft skin, and lightly kissed her on the neck. She leaned her head back onto my shoulder placing her hands on top of mine as I caressed her breasts. "We were made to be together," she whispered. I kissed her on the cheek still red from my hand.

"We are together."

18

Cheater came up to me in the school hallway first thing in the morning just before homeroom. I knew what she was going to talk about, and I honestly didn't have an answer for her. Then, she dropped the unexpected bomb on me.

"Whitney is missing," she said.

"What the fuck are you talking about?"

"Whitney's been missing since yesterday afternoon."

"I was with her yesterday, Cheater. You saw us standing in the rain, remember?" I snapped at her.

"I know, but her mother called my house after you left looking for her. She said she wanted to go for a walk, but she never came home."

"Meredith, you're scaring me."

"I'm telling you the truth. She's been reported missing." Thoughts raced around my mind. Where could she have gone, and why? David walked up and could see that I'd already heard the news from the town crier.

"What are we gonna do?" he asked as though I was the leader of the Merrimack River gang, and I made all the friggin' decisions. David looked over my head and saw Jonathan coming through the hallway doors with his friend Josh. I could tell they came from the smoking section of the school because of the smoke still lingering behind them.

He stopped in front of me and nodded his head. "We're here to help find Whit," he said, sticking his hand out to me. I shook it, putting our differences aside and instantly thought of a plan.

"How many of us can fit in your truck?" I asked, since there were five of us.

"Josh will take two, and I'll take—."

"I can't go," Cheater interrupted. "I have two tests today. Besides, if I skip school, I'll get suspended again."

"She's your friend, Meredith!" I shouted at her.

"I'm sorry, I can't. I just—."

"Whatever Cheater, we don't need your stupid excuses!" Jonathan spoke up. "Just leave, bitch."

Cheater squeezed her books against her chest and walked away.

"Okay, let's go," I said. "We'll stop at the dock and team up there."

I turned my head and looked down the crowded hallway and thought about when the best time to split from school would be before the hall monitor could spot us, when unexpectedly Jonathan whistled loud enough to ring everyone's ears in the hallway.

"Ditz!" he shouted. "Get your ass over here,

you're coming with us!" Ditz trotted over looking behind her searching for her other half. Then Jonathan whistled again, sending another ring through everyone's ears, and waved at Dotz to come over. One thing about Jonathan, he sure didn't give a rat's ass what people thought of him.

"Okay let's go," Jonathan said. "Ditz, you go with Josh, and Dotz, you come with me."

"What about that hallway bitch?" Josh asked pulling his keys out of his pocket.

"Fuck her," I said. Everyone looked at me and laughed.

We walked out of school right past the principal's office with our chins up, ready to take on the world heading toward the student parking lot when the principal himself shouted from the doorway. Jonathan looked back and stopped.

"Keep going. I'll tell him what's going on," he said to us.

Jonathan stopped in front of the boatyard and backed his truck into his usual spot next to his grandfather's old caddy. Josh parked his mom's car next to the Mako boat Jonathan's grandfather gave him when he turned fifteen.

We gathered inside the workshop where his grandfather was sleeping soundly in his old reclining chair in front of the black and white TV. I told everyone my plan. It wasn't much, but it was a start.

"David, Ditz, Dotz, and I will walk the river's

edge. Jonathan and Josh will scout out the road side. She couldn't have gone too far."

"What about the police?" Ditz asked.

"They don't know anything about our neighborhood," David snapped back.
"Besides, what the fuck are they going to do other than sit and wait for someone to call saying they found her dead. By then it'll be too late."

"He's right, Deanna," Dotz said softly.

"Let's go," Jonathan said. "And remember, if you find her, do the whistle. Dead or alive, do the whistle." Jonathan looked in everyone's eyes and stared at me as though there was more to it than just finding Whitney.

"Let's find your girl," he said, putting his hand out. For the second time that day we shook hands.

19

Hours had past; all of us were cold and tired searching every inch of the neighborhood for Whitney. We searched behind houses, trees, stone walls, and of course, Sewer Lane. I paid special attention around Sewer Lane hoping she hadn't killed herself, and then fallen into the cold icy water, never to be found . . .

Jonathan slowly drove up and down North Road and Middle Road searching both sides. The only thing he found was his old skate board someone had stolen from his back porch two years ago. Suddenly, we saw Josh flying up the road and slam on his brakes in front of Jonathan's truck. I watched from a distance as Josh jumped out of the car and ran over to Jonathan's window shouting and pointing his finger toward the old church on the corner of High Street and River Road. David and the girls looked at me. I looked at them with the same thoughts in my head, waiting for the whistle. Then the whistle was blown. Josh had found something, or her.

We gathered together on North Road listening to Josh. He told everyone there were clothes in the back of the old church, and we should check it out. I jumped into Jonathan's truck thinking she was beaten and raped, again, and then dragged somewhere else in the neighborhood to die. My hands were sweaty. I was scared.

When we pulled up to the church, I couldn't wait for Jonathan to stop the truck. I jumped out and fell flat on my face in the dirt. I ran toward the back, wiping my face, feeling the scratches on my cheek and saw the clothes bundled up against the rear door. I searched every inch of the clothes looking for some familiar shirt, or a pair of pants she wore. I tossed every stitch of clothing in every direction until I saw everyone looking down at me. My head was full of confusion. I didn't see anything of Whitney's that she wore. I was relieved, but yet I was still scared.

Ditz bent down and gave me a hug, holding me tight. Rummage sale clothes, I thought, remembering my mother had said they made enough money to put new doors on the church. Then, for some unknown reason, a strange thought had entered my mind. Maybe I was grasping at straws. Maybe something in my head just clicked. I don't know what happened, but it just happened.   "Roger Cass," I said in a low tone, looking up at David. Peter's much older trouble making brother. The one who believed he was Hercules and thought that he can walk around the neighborhood forcing other kids to do his dirty work, like breaking and entering into the old lady's house next to his and stealing her money for his drinking problem.

Finally, after three years of scaring the neighborhood and stealing money and jewelry, he got caught by Cliff McGowan's bad-tempered father. Cliff came home covered in dirt and showing off a big black eye because he refused to break into the Healey's house. From what everyone was told from Cliff's brother Sam, their father broke open the front door of Roger's house and smacked him around until Roger couldn't see anymore. He became quiet after that, real quiet for a long time.

"Roger," I said again. Everyone looked down at the Cass's mansion, two doors away from the old church.

"Peter's brother has her," I said softly. "That friggin' piece of shit"

"What made you think of that?" Jonathan asked.

"I don't know. Maybe it's because he'd always wanted to get into her pants."

"That doesn't mean shit," Josh spoke. "I've even said that."

"Yeah, but you're too stupid to do anything about it!" Ditz spoke loud enough to have her voice echo. "Christ, Josh, you've never even seen a real pair of tits!" she said, grabbing her own breasts.

"Fuck off, Ditz!"

"No, you fuck off, Josh!" Dotz yelled. "We're not just fuck trophies, ya know! We're people too!"

"Hey!" Jonathan shouted, stopping the argument before it escalated into a fist fight. "What do you want to do?" Jonathon asked me in a calm voice. "Do you want to call the police, or do you want to handle this by ourselves?" I looked at everyone waiting for my reply, thinking more and more about calling the police and letting them handle it, and then I thought, what if Roger didn't have anything to do with it? We would all look like a bunch of fools. Then again, why wouldn't he take revenge on Whitney? After all, her father did kill his brother.

"Let's do this by ourselves," I said, taking a deep nervous breath. Jonathan nodded.   I looked up at the sky knowing it was getting dark soon as we walked toward the Cass's house. I remembered when the Villenue's lived there years ago, and Brett showed me a secret room down in the dirt floored cellar where his father kept his collection of dirty reel to reel movies. When they moved far, far away, his mother asked me to take care of their Golden Retriever until they could come back to get him in a couple days. They never came back. Rusty became my dog and was twenty-one when he died. I missed him with all my heart.

David slid down the hill in the back of the Cass's house looking inside every dirty cellar window. I looked in every window after him, hoping I'd see something he might have missed. Jonathan, Josh and the girls knocked on the front door to distract anyone who was home from what we were doing. David tried the old gray paint chipped door leading into the cellar and opened it sending out a loud screeching noise from the rusty hinges. He looked at me, and then pushed the door open as fast as he could. It still squeaked loud enough to send an eerie chill up my spine like he just dragged his fingernails across a chalk board. David walked in and stepped on the damp dirt floor. I saw Jonathan walking toward me with his thumb up telling me that no one was home. I walked in the cellar looking around for the infamous secret room.

"It's over here," David whispered, opening the door slowly. My heart pounded like a hammer when he opened the door. I held my breath, trembling as I looked around the dark room and smelled the strong odor of mildew and dirty clothes.

Jonathan walked into the cellar as Josh and the girls stayed outside keeping guard. We looked around every inch of the dark cellar hoping for a miracle. Jonathan snapped his fingers at us and pointed up to the main door of the house. David walked toward him and followed him upstairs. I walked in the secret room again and clicked on the old light switch nailed to the exposed rotting beam near the rock foundation, which looked like it needed a major overhaul. When the light came on it was dull, very dull, but it was lit, and then I saw something familiar. Whitney's favorite painted gray sweatshirt lying on the floor. I swallowed hard as I picked it up thinking of the worst and put the sweatshirt against my face smelling the dampness of the cellar and her Baby Soft perfume. My hands began to shake with fear. For a brief moment, I gave up all hope I'd ever see her alive again. The nightmarish thought of finding her bones when the snow melted near the shore of the river rushed through my head.

"David!" I screamed and ran to the staircase. "David!" I yelled again even louder.

David came to the top of the steps gesturing me to stop yelling as I held up Whitney's sweatshirt. He ran down the stairs and looked at me with his eyes bugging out of his head. He looked into the secret room and pushed by me as though he knew something I didn't. He walked over to the paneled wall, then stuck his hand inside a small bite size hole and ripped open another secret door I didn't even know about, but he did. There she was, half naked; her breasts exposed with slash marks across her chest and stomach as though she had been whipped with a leather strap or a small branch. Her wrists were duct taped to a metal pole, and she was hanging with her feet barely touching the ground.

"Jesus," I whispered. She was in real pain. I could see it in her face. I could see everything through her eyes when she looked at me for a brief second. "Andy," she whispered in a frightened voice. "Please help me. He said he's going to kill me." I watched her slump her head down as though she died in front of me. I grabbed her by the waist.

20

Suddenly, Jonathan flew down the wooden stairs head first slamming his shoulders against every step. Roger Cass stomped after him in his dirty work boots, holding an aluminum baseball bat. David shook his head and pulled out his pocket knife, and tossed it to me landing on the ground inches from my foot

"I'll take care of Roger. You get Whitney the hell out of here," he told me. I nodded my head hearing the girls screaming. David ran toward Roger full force with his hands in the air and tried to block the swinging of the bat and took the brunt of a swing against his left shoulder. Jonathan got control of the bat and yanked it away from Roger. He tossed it against the rock foundation, and fell into the wet dirt floor

Jonathan and David then wrestled with the devil for minutes that felt like hours, dragging him out through the cellar door, when Ditz quickly picked up a big rock next to the doorway, and bashed it against Roger's head, knocking him unconscious. Jonathan and David stopped in total shock, breathing heavy. They looked at Ditz with wonder.

"Nice job, Ditz," David said.

"I just hope you didn't kill him," Jonathan stated.

"Why not," Dotz asked with no expression. "He deserves to die, just like his rapist brother."

I cut the tape away from Whitney's wrists as she fell against me. I carried her half naked body backwards out the door, with her feet dragging on the ground, feeling her somewhat warm skin on my hands that gave me a sense of relief knowing she was still alive, and then laid her down in the cold snow. Her eyes opened up in a state of shock and jumped up crossing her arms. When her eyes focused on me, she lunged toward me at full force knocking me down to the ground.

"I'm here," I said, holding her tight. "I'm here."

"I'm going to call the police," Jonathan, said taking a deep breath. He put his hand on David's shoulder. Whitney looked at Roger still knocked out on the ground with a small spot of blood that covered the top of his head.

"He said he was going to kill me because my father killed his brother," Whitney said, pulling away from me. Ditz quickly took her coat off and wrapped it around Whitney.

"Are you okay?" I asked. She looked at me with her eyes filled with tears and nodded her head.

"I'm okay, really." She said slipping her

arms into the coat. Roger started to move around on the ground, when Ditz picked up the same rock and hit him in the head again. "He's not getting away this time," she said, holding the rock like she was ruler of ancient Valencia. For that one moment in life, we all just simply smiled.

I walked back in the cellar to pick up Whitney's favorite sweatshirt, and then pressed it against my face one more time before I handed it to her. We heard a police car pull up in front of the house.

"Over here!" I shouted. Then another cruiser skid its tires to a stop. In the distance, we heard sirens blaring. "Here comes the Cavalry," Dotz said.

Two police officers came running over just as Roger started moving again. Dotz and Ditz pointed their finger at Roger telling the officers he was the one who kidnapped Whitney. One of the officers slammed his knee down on his back and handcuffed his hands before Roger even had a chance to think.

"Lock him away forever!" Dotz yelled and spit in Roger's face. Whitney looked at me and grabbed my hand. "Take me home," she said in my ear. "Take me home."

"Miss Williams, you can't go anywhere until we get a statement from you, and have you checked out at the hospital," the police officer said, pulling Roger off the wet ground.

"I'm fine. I don't need to go to the hospital."

"It's in your best interest. You must get checked out."

"No!" Whitney shouted. "I'm fine."

Whitney's mother ran over in hysterics and hugged her as though she'd been missing for years. The new police officer, which none of us has ever seen before, asked all of us the same questions they asked Jonathan in the front of the house.

Whitney walked away with her mother holding her tight. Her mother turned her head and looked at me. She didn't say anything to me, she just looked as though I was the cause of all this. Whitney put her head against her mother's shoulder. We all watched until she sat in the back of the rescue squad. Again, her mother looked at us. Ditz had a strange look in her eye like she was thinking the same thing I was. I should have seen it coming because since that day, everything had changed for the worse.

David walked over to me and held his hand out. I pulled his pocket knife out of my pocket and handed it to him. He nodded his head and wrapped his arm around Ditz looking at Jonathan, waiting for his smart remarks. Maybe Jonathan did care, but that day he didn't dare to show it, at least not around us.

21

That February, a horrific blizzard came through dropping more than three feet of snow. Tree branches the size of drainage pipes broke like twigs. There was no sign of anybody after Roger Cass kidnapped Whitney. Not even David. I suspected he'd been hanging around with that piece of shit Luke again smoking pot. According to the school grapevine, he was caught stealing money and cigarettes from lockers and was suspended for three days.

Meredith usually stood in front of her bedroom window, but on this day, she wasn't there. I remembered last year she told me she hated the snow. After the huge nor'easter that kept us out of school for nearly a week, I decided I hated snow more than she did. As for my friend Randy, well, you won't ever see him during the winter. He's a goddamn ski machine hanging around Killington, Vermont, flying down the mountain at a hundred miles an hour. People say when he skis, he comes down so fast it looks like he's flying.

I walked down the street to my friend Derek's house to talk to his stepfather, John Richard Parry about Whitney's amazing paintings.

John, Jr. and his younger sister Diane, who had special needs, had come to live with their dad John Parry after their mother admitted herself into a rehabilitation hospital for being addicted to pain killers. Two years later she killed herself and her boyfriend, but John Jr. and his sister were not told until John turned eighteen. Diane didn't totally understand about death.

As I approached the door, I heard the sound of arguing. It sounded like Mr. Parry and his wife were really going at it. I knocked on the door anyway and waited. I didn't think anyone heard the knocking over the yelling, so I knocked even louder. Finally, John answered the door with a smile as though I saved him from losing the argument.

"Derek's not here. He's at his father's this weekend in Gloucester," he said.

"I'm not here for Derek," I told him. "I'm here to talk to you."

"He doesn't have time to talk, you little twerp. Come back later!" Derek's mother shouted from the background. Derek told me sometime ago she was psychotic. I never believed him until now. John opened the door wider rolling his eyes, and stepped out of the house shutting the door behind him. "What's up?" he asked, putting his hands in his pockets. He had deep brown eyes, a graying beard, and a handlebar mustache waxed to a thin point. His face seemed a little thin. I remember looking at him that day, thinking to myself, "Someday he's going to leave Derek's mother and never look back." He finally did years later and seemed happier for it.

"I want to talk to you about Whitney Williams," I said.

"Nice looking girl," He said smiling broadly. "She has the most beautiful hair I've ever seen."

"She's an artist, a painter," I said.

"Is she good?" he asked after a long pause.

"John," I said softly. "When I saw her latest painting, I thought you had done it." He nodded, no longer smiling.

"When can I see some of her work?" he asked.

"I'll go see if she's home." I left his house and walked down the street filled with excitement. John stood outside for the longest time watching me walk up the hill toward Whitney's house.

22

In my excitement, I figured it would be faster to cut through the woods to Whitney's house. I soon found myself in snow waist deep and swearing at the shitty weather that never seems to go away. I managed to knock on the door of Whitney's house and bang the snow off my boots at the same time. My banging sounded like the whole porch was breaking down. Whitney opened the door wearing her usual ugly pajamas. Before I could speak, I saw a much older man come up behind her and wrap his tree-trunk sized arm around her shoulders. I stared at her.

"Tell me this isn't real," I said. She started to protest, but I wouldn't let her talk.
"You wanted us to be together," I said through gritted teeth. "You're throwing it away with this? Fuck you, Whitney!" I turned away before she could say a word. As I stormed off, I was grabbed by the back of my coat, and tossed to the icy driveway. The guy she was with stepped on my chest and pressed down so hard I could barely breathe.
"Jimmy, don't hurt him!" Whitney shouted. "He doesn't know who you are!" This strange man

stared at me for a moment and then lifted his size fourteen shoe off my chest. I turned onto my side coughing up a lung and finally catching my breath. "What the fuck?!" I screamed.

"Honey," Whitney said in a soft calm tone as she walked toward me, and then helped me up off the cold ground. I stood there still trying to breathe normal, holding my hand against my chest and looked at her, feeling so hurt and jealous. And feeling such hatred that I wanted to kill her.

"This is Jimmy," she explained. "He's my older brother. He and his wife are here to visit for a couple of weeks. They live in Anchorage, Alaska."

Jimmy slapped his gorilla hand against my back, almost knocking the wind out of me again. He smiled and stuck his hand out. I didn't want to shake his hand fearing I'd never get it back, but I did, and it hurt. Again, I hated him even more, but I forced a smile and a nod. Whitney grinned at me with a slight giggle, and then kissed me ever so gently on the lips. "I've missed you," she said. "Where have you been?" I felt like an ass now that I knew who Bigfoot was.

"I called, but your mother kept telling me you weren't around," I told her.

"Ha! That's mom for ya!" Jimmy said, laughing as he walked toward the house.

"Let's go inside. It's cold out here." She wrapped her arm around my neck and squeezed me harder than I would ever imagine, feeling somewhat shocked at her strength. As I walked in the house, her mother was there in the kitchen chugging on a bottle of red wine. Think you can use a glass, I thought, but didn't say out loud. "Whitney, we need to talk," I said in a serious tone. She looked at me as though she knew what I was going to say. I saw the tears in her eyes instantly fill up and then stream down her face.

"Say it," she said fisting her hands together. I knew she'd become a little more sensitive since the nightmare at the drive-in, but this was a little too much.

Suddenly, she snapped her hand across my throat, slammed me against the wall, and stared deep into my eyes.

"Okay," I paused for a long moment thinking she was going to punch me or choke me. "John Parry wants to see your paintings." I said gasping for air. "I told him about your work and how great they are."

Whitney instantly released her squeezing grip and stepped back from me just as her mother came dashing into the hallway. She was wearing a red shirt with a stupid homemade baby face made from nylon stuck to the front of it. What the hell is that? I wondered.

"You know John?" she asked looking at me pinned against the wall.

"Yes." I wondered why she was listening to our conversation. I rubbed my neck feeling the indents where Whitney's nails dug into me.

"Whitney, this is your chance to really make it!" She shouted with joy. "Oh my God," she shouted even louder, wrapping her arms around Whitney.

"Isn't that Derek's stepfather?" Whitney asked. "I thought he worked at the Portsmouth Naval shipyard?"

"Whitney," her mother spoke with excitement. "He's a well-known Marine artist. He's painted murals for President's. He's made paintings for celebrities. Whitney, go downstairs and get some pictures together!"

"Mom, will you calm down. Go have another drink or something." She snapped. Whitney and I watched Jimmy lightly grab his mother's arm; pull her to the kitchen, telling her we wanted to talk alone.

"What do you say, Whit? You wanna have John look at those paintings of yours?"

"So, you're not breaking up with me?" she asked. I put my hand on her beautiful face, wiping the wetness from her cheek and thought about her hand around my neck.

"I never would have dreamed of breaking up with you. Why would you even think that? We're together you and me, and that's that." Whitney jumped at me, hugged me until I almost went numb. "I love you forever," she whispered in my ear. What I wanted to hear was I'm sorry for grabbing and squeezing your throat. But that never came.

"I love you too," I said. "Now, Whitney, what about those paintings we can show John?"

In answer, she walked to the basement door and down the steep stairs, flicking the light on with her foot. She waited until I stepped on the last step, and then wrapped her arms around me again.

"Make love to me," she said unbuttoning her pajama top. "I need you. I want you."

I wanted her too in the worst way, but I didn't want to be swayed from our purpose at hand. "Let's just call John first, okay? See if he's available. Then..."

"Okay," she said, buttoning her pajama top. She seemed a little put out but not too bad. "I'll get some of the paintings together." I turned to go back upstairs to the phone when she blurted out, "I want to have your baby." I continued up the stairs pretending I didn't hear. But I was scared. I wasn't ready to be a father, not yet.

I picked up the phone and dialed Derek's number. Fortunately, John picked up. I asked him if he had time for us to come over with the artwork. He answered, but my mind was still on Whitney's comment.

"I'm sorry, what?" I asked.

"Tomorrow would be better for me," John replied for the second time. That time I heard him. "Okay, tomorrow then. I'll help Whitney get her stuff together, and we'll come down around two o'clock?" I said.

"That's fine," he replied and hung up the phone without saying goodbye.

I hung up the phone with Whitney's little surprise still on my mind. I wanted to go down and act like nothing was said, but when she came up the stairs, she was holding her stomach like she was going to be sick.

"What's the matter?" I asked. She looked at me holding back a smile and fixed her eyes on her mother gulping down the last of her wine bottle. "I think I'm pregnant again," she whispered. I didn't say anything.

"The only person I've been with since Peter raped me is you." She looked at me wondering what my reaction was going to be. I stood there like a bump on a log. I had to tell her I was too young. My mother told me one day, if I get a girl in the motherly way, my life was over, so don't screw up. "Whit—"

"But I think maybe I have a stomach bug because it feels a lot different than before," she said . A knock at the door interrupted us. Whitney walked over and opened the door halfway and saw the police standing on the old porch. Sergeant David Vance stepped in before Whitney could invite him.

"Can I help you?" she asked stepping back.

"I need to ask you some questions if you don't mind." He replied. I stood there in the sidelines watching him ask Whitney some questions about her best friend Meredith.

What the hell did Cheater do now? I wondered. Whitney looked at me as though she needed help. Sergeant David Vance took his hat off and turned toward me.

"What," I asked.

"When was the last time you saw Meredith K. Chandler?" he asked, staring directly into my eyes. He made me nervous. He looked at me as though I had done something awful. Why don't you just shoot me now, and ask questions later, I thought sarcastically.

"I don't know, couple weeks ago," I answered, but I was pretty much guessing since I really didn't care whether I talked to her or not. "Why?"

"She's dead, isn't she?" Whitney stated. "And you're walking around the neighborhood asking questions." Whitney snapped. Sergeant Vance looked at her trying to be professional. "No, but she was rushed to the hospital last night." Whitney and I looked at each other, wondering the same thing.

"What happened?" Whitney asked. Sergeant Vance paused for a brief moment as though he was not going to answer the question.

"What happened to Cheater?" I shouted loud enough for Whitney's mother to walk into the hallway.

"She tried to commit suicide," he said addressing Whitney ignoring me. "Her father told me you're her best friend, so I came here to ask you if she might have said anything to you within the last couple of days."

"Meredith would have told me if something was bothering her. She always did."

"Apparently not this time," her mother spoke.

"How are you doing lately, Barbara?" Sergeant Vance asked, trying to keep a straight face.

"I'm hanging in there." She replied, waving her hand around in a circle.

"Yeah, how's Richie doing?" he asked, smirking a little bit.

"What's that supposed to mean?"

"It didn't mean anything."

"Bullshit," Barbara shouted. "He was screwing the next door neighbor's wife, so I started screwing Richie, is that what you wanted to hear?"

"Barbara, that's none of my--"

"That's Ms. Williams now. The bastard is dead, remember?"

"Mom!" Whitney shouted, rushing by me almost pushing me into the wall, and then ran up the stairs to her room.

"Barbara, I think you've had a little too much to drink. You need to go lie down."

"You know what I think, Mr. Policeman. I think you should get the fuck out of my house." Sergeant Vance watched her swaying back and forth, and then looked at me.

"It's quite clear I'm not getting any answers around here," he said in a low tone. "Barbara, why don't you go suck on another bottle," He shouted opening the door and stomping out.

"Why don't you go arrest somebody for jay-walking......Asshole!" she slammed the front door, then looked at me like she wanted to grab the back of my neck and toss me out too.

"What are you looking at, you little piss ant? I know why you're here, you little, horny bastard. Did you fuck my daughter yet?"

I didn't answer. Whitney's mother stumbled into the kitchen again and pulled out one of the kitchen chairs dragging it hard over the tile floor. I didn't know whether she was holding the chair for balance, or she was going to hit me with it.

"Jimmy!" she shouted, slamming her fist against the table. "Jimmy, where the hell are you? Goddamn it!" I looked in the living room and saw Jimmy sitting peacefully on the couch with a pair of headphones on, listening to the music.

Whitney was sobbing, face down on her bed, when I walked into the room. I looked out the window and saw the dog's body was still there, frozen into the ground. "Jesus," I whispered.

"What," Whitney answered.

"Whit, what happened to your dog?"

"I got mad one day and killed it. I imagined it was Peter and shot it right between the ears. I hated that dog; it never stopped barking."

"I have to go," I said quickly, heading for the door. Whitney jumped up and blocked me before I could leave.

"Make love to me. Right now, I want you to

stay with me. I want your love." She began frantically unbuttoning her top. I grabbed her hands and squeezed them tight. "I'm leaving," I told her. "I don't want to have sex with you right now. I want to go home. I want you to get some of your paintings together, so we can show John tomorrow." Whitney's eyes turned mean, and she stared at me as though she thought of shooting me through the head. She ripped her hands away from mine, and slapped me across the face as hard as she could. I lost my balance and landed on the floor just inches from the bed post. My face felt like a nest of bees stinging me.

"You're not going anywhere! You're staying here!" she screamed and came over to me. She grabbed the back of my hair.

"You will fuck me like the whore i am," she demanded. I felt her finger nails digging into the back of my scalp pulling me up until I sat on the bed. Then she calmly let go of my hair and smiled as if nothing had happened. She took a deep breath and finished unbuttoning her pajama top. She slipped off her bottoms and stood in front of me with nothing on but her red bikini underwear.

"What are you waiting for, honey? Take off your clothes."

I put my head down. I felt like a turtle in a fish tank—trapped and drowning. Whitney placed her arms around my head and pressed my face between her breasts.

"I love you with all my heart," she said,

squeezing me even tighter. I shoved her away and ran for the door. Whitney lunged at me, slamming me against the wall, and reached for a pair of scissors on top of her bureau.

"What are you going to do, Whitney?" I asked. She pressed the scissors against my neck, stiff armed, pushing the point into my skin, and bit down hard on her teeth, drooling off the corner of her mouth.

"Please don't," I pleaded closing my eyes. Whitney dropped the scissors to the floor and covered her mouth with her hands.

"Oh my God!" she shouted. "Baby, I'm sorry. I don't know what came over me." She looked down at her breasts and wrapped her arms around them. I walked over and picked up her pajama top and handed it to her.

"I think you need some rest, Whitney. You look tired." I told her, taking a deep breath feeling my neck to see if she struck any blood.

She nodded and dressed. "I don't know what happened to me," she said running her hand through her hair. She looked confused and embarrassed, but I still watched everything she did for a moment until she calmly sat on the bed. I backed out of her bedroom and ran down the stairs and out the front door. When I finally stopped running, I was in front of Meredith's house. I caught my breath and then realized I'd left my coat on the old coat rack next to the staircase.

I walked home, my arms turning to ice.

23

I called David's house, since I haven't seen him. I wanted to tell him about Whitney and her little crazy side I never saw before until yesterday. My mother told me she had seen David uptown in front of the Richdale's convenience store a few days earlier just hanging with a bunch of kids. I knew what he was doing, and I knew our friendship had taken a turn for the worse. I decided to go look for him, although I wasn't sure that I'd even wanted to find him now.

I made it to the windy bridge and saw Jonathan's truck coming down the road at top speed. He stopped in front of me with a long skid, as usual. His Tweedle's were nowhere in the truck. I wasn't surprised, but I was also curious. Maybe they did finally get fed up with him. Maybe they said that's that. I hoped so.

"They don't come around anymore, and they don't call either," he said, somehow guessing what I was thinking about. *Good,* I thought.

"Where's David?" I asked him.

"Hop in. I'll give you a ride down to where he is."

Jonathan drove down the street in a normal fashion all the way to Luke's house where there were a bunch of cars in the driveway and on the side of the road. One of which was a nice Camaro Hotrod from that spoiled, rich high school senior Justin Smith that we all hated. His father built it for him, probably from petty cash. The rest of the cars there were just average.

"What's going on?" I asked.

"Luke is having a pot party," he explained. "This is where David's been hanging out lately."

"How come you're not here?" I had to ask since he was in with the "crowd." Jonathan put the truck in park, leaned against the seat and looked at me, and then shook his head. As much as he wanted to tell me to get the hell out, he didn't. Not after he told me he changed his ways some time ago.

"I don't do any of that shit anymore. I quit cold turkey." I was shocked. I couldn't believe it. I was happy for him, He was still an asshole

"What made you change?" I asked him. He looked out the passenger window and saw Luke, the chubby spare tire kid walking toward us.

"I got to go," he said. "You need to get out." I jumped out of the truck, and he drove up the road before Luke made it to the end of the driveway.

"That chicken shit," Luke shouted, wiping his nose.

Tweedle Ditz, and her side kick Dotz came out of the house. They looked at me and smiled.

I hadn't seen either of them since we found Whitney in the Cass' house, but for some reason, Dotz looked better than usual. She was wearing her purple coat, tied at the waist showing off her sexy curves, and her hair was blonde. It complemented her crystal blue eyes.

"Hey," I said. I could smell the strong odor of the illegal herb when they came closer. "You look nice, Dorothy." She smiled and tilted her head when I called her by her proper name.
She winked at me, but she didn't say anything. She didn't need to. I looked at Luke thinking he's getting these nice girls in trouble. He's such a piece of shit.

"I have to go," I said, walking away. I looked one more time at Dottie's curves, wondering what she looked like underneath that purple coat and smiled a fake smile.

"Your pussy David is not here anyway, so keep walking!" Luke shouted at me.

"Yeah, okay, Luke. Whatever asshole," I said sarcastically

I walked a little past Whitney's house still thinking about Dottie, and David's bad habit. I was cold, alone, and miserable. I saw Richie getting out of his truck with a brown paper bag. He looked at me with a shitty look, and then went in the house. I suddenly felt that eerie feeling that someone was watching me. I looked up at Whitney's window, and there she was, staring down at me like she was a crazy woman in a psyche ward. I waved at her walking toward her door but stopped before I stepped on the old porch. I was still more than a little freaked out by what happened last week. Whitney opened the door with her eyes sparkling in the sun wearing a smile from ear to ear. She was wearing a beautiful white sleeveless dress with her hair styled to perfection, and a small but elegant bow clipped in the back. She looked wonderful. She looked incredible. She looked like the girl I fell in love with. Hopefully she wasn't in that crazy violent mood she was in the last time I saw her. Jesus, she scared the shit out of me that day.

"Hi," she said. I opened my arms to her, and she jumped in. Her mother stood quietly behind her, watching us.

"Did you show your paintings to John?" I asked her. She hugged me tighter, ignoring the question. I took it as a no answer, but I also gave myself another mental note to bring John here instead but when? That was the hardest part.

I sensed something amiss. Something was wrong. Then her mother spoke up. "Whitney, we need to go see your doctor in a little while. You and your so-called boyfriend can spend a little time together upstairs until we need to go."

"Do you want to come see what I did to my room?" Whitney asked, still holding that perfect smile.

"Sure." I said as she took a soft hold of my hand.

Doctor? I thought. *What kind of doctor?*

She led me into her house, and the first thing I saw hanging on the coat rack was my other coat I had been scared to come and get. I unzipped my coat, and quickly slipped it off hanging it over my other one, so I made sure I wouldn't forget it this time for any reason. We walked upstairs. I could feel her mother's eyes glued to me, burning into my back. My eyes widened when I saw her room. She had painted the walls a soft pink and pasted a border around the top.

"You like?" she asked smiling from ear to ear.

"I like it a lot!" I said. I looked at her and saw an expensive pearl necklace around her neck. She caught me looking and followed her finger up and down the pearls. "It was my grandmother's," she said. "Honey, I'm real sorry about the other day. I didn't mean to scare you like that."

"That's okay," I said and walked to the window over looking the pool thinking of the dog she killed. I looked down at the doghouse and was relieved that the dog's corpse was gone. Then I noticed another dog sitting inside the house. It was a nice looking golden retriever about a year old.

"Did you get a new dog?" I asked, thinking how long that one has to live before the sharp shooter puts a hole in it.

"Yes. His name is Taz, after the character in *Bugs Bunny*. Do you want me as much as I want you?" She asked, jumping off the subject, and sliding her soft hand down my back giving me a chill up my spine. I wanted her in the worst way, but I knew she was going to see her doctor in a little while, and the thought of having her mother walk in on us when it was time to go wasn't something I wanted to experience.

"We don't have time," I told her. She wrapped her arms around me giving me a kiss on the neck and stared out the window in silence. We both jumped at the sound of a loud scream coming from downstairs.

24

It didn't sound like a woman's scream. It didn't sound like her mother. It didn't sound familiar at all. Then I remembered Richie was downstairs. Whitney suddenly ran out of her room and flew down the stairs so fast; I didn't even get the chance to turn around.

I ran down the stairs and stopped at the bottom step and saw Richie covered in blood with deep slices across his face, his chest, and arms. He was bleeding profusely. Whitney's mother was holding a butcher knife with blood all over it, and Whitney was struggling to take it from her. I ran toward Whitney to help her grab the knife away when Richie fell against the wall and slid down to the floor. Whitney punched her mother square in the face and knocked her unconscious. At the same time, her brother Bigfoot Jimmy came stomping up the basement stairs and slammed open the door, causing the handle to puncture the wall

"What happened?" He shouted.

"I don't know, but Richie is bleeding to death. Call the ambulance!" I screamed. Jimmy ran

Andrew LeBel

into the kitchen and dialed 911. Whitney stood over her mother like a gladiator who just won the battle killing her opponent and grabbed the butcher knife from her hand. I didn't do anything, I couldn't. All I could do is look down at Richie, wondering whether or not he was going to die right in front of me. Jimmy ran back with a wet cloth and pressed it against Richie's face to try to stop the bleeding.

"Go get some more wet cloths!" he shouted. I looked at Whitney as I ran into the kitchen looking for anything that even resembled a cloth. Whitney walked ever so calmly into the kitchen like she was in a fog, threw the bloody knife into the sink, opened up the closet near the refrigerator, and pulled out a bundle of hand towels. She went to the sink, soaked them dripping wet, and walked back out to the hallway and gave her brother the towels. We heard the blaring sirens coming closer. I opened the door feeling the cold air and saw the ambulance stopping in the middle of the road with a police car behind it. Jimmy was still pressing the towels against Richie's face and arms.
I jumped out of the way when the paramedics rushed in with a stretcher. Whitney's beautiful dress was splattered with blood. But she didn't seem to notice or care.

As the paramedics took Richie away strapped to the bed, the police pulled Whitney's mother off

114

the floor and arrested her for assault and battery with a dangerous weapon with intent to kill.

I stood outside out of the way and watched the ambulance drive away, thinking this is getting to be just another usual day at the William's house. I looked at the yellow house across the street and saw the shadow of the old woman through the curtain in the window.   Whitney came outside and crossed her arms looking at me. My arms couldn't have wrapped around her fast enough. Her brother came out and put his hand on Whitney's back and told her he was staying a little bit longer than he expected.

"Where did you learn to punch like that?" I asked her.

"Self defense tapes," she said with a smile. "My mother got them at the store for me a few days after you rescued me from Roger Cass. I said to her, that's enough, I want to take fighting lessons, but I never thought I'd actually use it, especially on Mom."

Whitney never went to see her doctor that day. Matter of fact, the only thing she did was, take my hand, escort me into the house, and up to her room where I helped unzip her blood splattered dress.

The next day, Cheater called me.

"Hey, Cheater, I mean Meredith, what's going on?"

"Hey, I just want to tell you something before you hear something else from rumor Ville."

"What?"

"I-I just wanted to tell you, that I didn't overdose on sleeping pills. They were put in my drink on purpose, and the only person that could have done that was Whitney."

"That's impossible." I told her. "I was with Whitney the same time she was taken away in the ambulance."

"She was over my house to get a book from me. I went upstairs to get it. That's when I figured she slipped in the pills."

"That's bullshit!" I shouted loud enough to have my mother come in the kitchen and yell at me for swearing.

"Why would she do that to her best friend?" I asked her. That's when Cheater told me the real story. They haven't been best friends since she set her up with Peter Cass. They haven't really spoken at all.

"She blames me for Peter raping her," she said. I was speechless. Now I could understand why Whitney was so angry but to try to kill Cheater was too much to comprehend.

"I told Peter to take advantage of her, but I never told him to rape her." I didn't say anything. I couldn't. In my mind, and Whitney's, she had Peter rape her.

"You're nothing but a piece of shit, Cheater!" I shouted again. My mother grabbed the phone from my hand and hung it up. At that point after saying those words, it was a perfect way to end the conversation. I was banned from using the phone for two weeks.

25

David unexpectedly came in the house that afternoon wearing his father's waders and a strange looking hat. "You ready?" he asked. I went upstairs without saying a word and put my waders on and walked outside. David came out behind me.

"Where the hell have you been?" I asked.

"I've been hanging out with Luke."

"Why? He's an asshole."

"I'm going out with his sister," he said. I tried not to laugh. I turned my head away and looked at Cheater's house with her standing in the window. David followed my eyes. "Did you hear what she did?" he asked me.

"I heard," I replied, assuming he was talking about Whitney.

"That bitch called the police on Luke and told them he was selling weed to everyone in school."

"Really?" I asked, but inside I was thinking it was about time.

"She had Whitney raped," I blurted out. David looked at me in shock, but he didn't say anything. He knew I would explain sometime, but right now, he knew I wanted to forget about life for a while and spend some time with my best friend.

Sewer Lane was totally frozen after the whole month of February's frigid temperatures. We walked down on the ice anyway and followed the brook to the mouth. We looked out over the open river that stretched across to West Newbury more than a football field away. We walked out testing the thickness of the ice, and before we knew it, we were standing in the middle of the river.

I looked at the shores of West Newbury and at the old house where supposedly a murder had taken place. It was boarded up with signs plastered all over the outside of the house that said "Do not enter." I looked at David the same time he looked at me. We both had the same thought. We crossed the river to the house.

"Pull the board off the door," I said. David grabbed the board and pulled with all his might and yanked the board off, at the same time he lost his balance and fell down the stairs into the snow. I laughed and helped him up. We opened the door and saw furniture covered with white sheets, and layers of dust on the floor. The air was stale. I lifted the white sheet covering the couch, looking for dried blood or some other signs of murder.

David started walking up the rugged covered staircase, leaving his wet footprints on each step. I had the feeling that someone was watching us looking at every wood-covered window. "This is creepy," I said.

"Hey," David whispered from the top of the stairs. "Come up and check these paintings out.
I joined him and saw a painting of a man holding a golden sword.

"Wow," I said in awe.

"Look higher," David said, pointing his finger over the picture.

"The golden sword," I whispered. "Reach up and grab it." David reached up and tipped the sword off the rack with his fingers. The sword fell to the floor, the clanging echoing through the hallway. We both froze. I wondered if someone had heard the noise and if we were going to get caught. I picked up the heavy sword, and carefully slid my palm over the dusty blade.

"Wow, David, look at this beauty," I said. "I'm taking this thing home." David just smiled.

We walked around looking in every room, wondering what kind of people lived here. David gestured me to come into the master bedroom. There was a locked wooden trunk at the end of a canopied bed. David pried open the lock with the fireplace poker. Inside the trunk were newspapers dating from 1920s. I lifted one of the papers and saw some old stuff underneath. "Costume jewelry," I said.

"Is it?" David asked, putting the necklaces, bracelets, and rings in his pocket.

"David, let's get out of here," I said and headed for the door when suddenly we heard the downstairs door open and close.

26

We both slid under the bed and peaked out through the bed skirt hanging down to the floor. We waited, and waited, and waited. Nothing, no sounds of anyone walking down the hall, no sounds of anyone breathing, but still we waited.

Close to four hours passed before we dared to even move. Finally, we crept out from under the bed and looked out the window. No one was around. I listened at the door but heard nothing.

"Hey, let's go," I whispered. David and I tiptoed down the hallway stopping every time we made even the slightest creek noise, and waited to hear somebody, or anybody coming up the stairs.

When we finally made it to the front door, we looked out and noticed there were fresh tire tracks that stopped near the front steps and footprints in the snow other than ours. We looked in every direction, and then ran to the river sliding down the banking and buried ourselves in the snow. I was still holding the sword. We stayed there until we knew for sure the coast was clear. We were cold, scared, and wanted to go home, but home was more than a hundred yards away, or if we walked around to the Rocks Village Bridge it was six miles away. In the frigid temperature, it would have felt like a thousand miles.

"You ready?" David asked me.

"Let's go." We ran across the frozen river as fast as we could with the waders on, feeling the ice cracking under our feet. We jumped onto the frozen shore line, dashed into the mouth of Sewer Lane, and stopped just near the old bridge to catch our breath. We made it across without getting caught. We made it without falling through the ice and drowning. We made it, period. We looked across the river at the old house, and we both fell down laughing. Then we saw the West Newbury police cruiser stopped on the side of the road looking at us. Next, we saw the Merrimac police cruiser stopping on the side of the road next to Sewer Lane. The cop jumped out of the cruiser and walked down the embankment toward us. I quickly slid the golden sword under the ice next to the base of the bridge. David emptied his pockets in the same spot. The officer looked at us with a smile. I looked at David.

"Shit," I whispered. "We didn't make it."

"Hello, boys."

27

Mud season was upon us, the season before the beginning of spring, and just before the end of winter. The snow melts almost all at once causing the ground to become very soft, and of course, muddy. We New Englanders love this season because it tells us we can start breathing again. And David and I loved it because it was the best time to float on the ice on Sewer Lane.

David was walking down the street with his waders on. He had been grounded from the whole incident at the old house, but was free again as was I. The cops never found the jewels or the sword we stole, and we hadn't been able to go back to retrieve them.

I walked out of the house with my waders on and saw David walking up the driveway. He didn't look happy.

"What's your problem?" I asked.

"Nothing, I'm just sick of my father's shit."

"What did he say now?"

"Nothing, just forget it." I knew when to let things go.

We made it down to Sewer Lane, taking the

long way around so we wouldn't have to walk by Whitney's house and have her ask me to come in.

David broke the ice and dug into the mud next to the old bridge pulling out the golden sword and handed it to me. Then he found all the jewels and placed them on the ice. The gold lion's ring is what he liked the best. For the first time in a long time, I saw David genuinely smile. I washed the sword in the polluted water and noticed something strange about it. I realized it was made in the thirteenth century by the style of the handle, and the engraving written on the sword itself.

"Oh shit, David," I yelled.

"What," he asked.

"This sword is worth some serious money!"

"So?" he said, shrugging his shoulders. I could have slapped him in the head. I wanted to slap him, but he was standing too far away, so I threw a piece of ice at him.

"So? What are you, stupid?" I was so excited, I almost peed myself. I ran my hand across the steel blade imagining the history it held, the people it had killed. I wondered how on earth it got here.

"You ready?" David asked. I looked at him not thinking about anything else but the sword.

"Are you ready to float on the ice, dumb ass?"

"Yeah, I'm ready," I said and carefully leaned the sword against the old bridge.

We floated around for hours until the tide started coming, threatening to cover our stolen

Andrew LeBel

goods. David jumped off the biggest piece of ice left on Sewer Lane and waded to shore. As I watched him sloshing through the thick black mud, I got tangled up in a low hanging branch and fell head first into the water. It was cold, but thank god it wasn't cold enough to freeze. I walked to the shore wiping my face, listening to David laughing at me while I flipped him the bird.

David handed me the sword. I slid it down inside my water filled waders. I looked up and saw Jonathan standing on the bridge watching us. I hoped he didn't see me with the sword. I walked up the muddy bank embankment to meet him.

"Hey," I said, looking around for his beat up truck. Jonathan looked at me funny as though he was going to tell me something, but he didn't know how. I looked down at David trying to climb up the bank, slipping down every step he made. I figured since he laughed the whole time I was in the water, he could drag his sorry ass up by himself.

"Hey," Jonathan said, looking at David.

"What's the matter?" I asked.

"Dude, its friggin' Whitney, man."

"What now?" I asked. David walked over stomping his feet on the black top, with his hands inside his waders still trying to slide the jewelry in his pockets.

"I don't know, man. I think you should go and see for yourself." Jonathan pointed his finger to his truck parked across the street on the dirt road

126

running parallel with Sewer Lane. We called it the cutoff because the Gulezians made a path through the woods, right into their driveway.

We jumped into the back of his truck feeling the bumps in the road. I stood up, holding on to the roof because of the sword in my pants, feeling the chilly air on my face. David stood next to me.

When we turned the corner toward Whitney's house, Jonathan stopped at the top of the hill and slammed the truck into park.

"Lots of shit has been going on down there lately," he said.

We stared at her house for a while in silence when Meredith walked out of her house. She was barely dressed and had no coat on.

"Oh shit," I said out loud. David jumped down off the truck, and I still stood there staring at Whitney's house, trying to ignore Cheater and wondered what Jonathan was talking about.

"Get out, dumb ass!" Jonathan yelled at me.

"Bite me, you piece of shit!" I yelled back and jumped off the truck. Right then and there, I knew we were back to our normal hateful ways again. It didn't bother me because that's just the way we were to each other, always.

"Good luck with the psychopath," Jonathan said as he jumped into his truck. As usual, He slammed his truck into gear with his foot on the gas and burned his tires into the pavement leaving a nice long black mark reaching passed Whitney's driveway. Meredith watched Jonathan leave and shook her head.

"Such an asshole," she said. I could see her nipples poking out of her flimsy T-shirt and knew David was looking as well.

"Whitney had the police at her house again," Meredith said, crossing her arms against her chest. She knew we were looking at her.

"Jesus Christ. Again? Why?" I asked.

"I don't know."

"Maybe it's because of her mother trying to kill Richie?"

I looked at David, still staring at Cheater's chest. I pushed him enough to lose his balance and get him out of his little trance he was in.

"What the hell?" he said, pushing me back.

"Snap out of it!" I shouted.

"Hey, you guys wanna come inside and hang out?" Meredith asked, pulling her shirt down more.

"Okay," David said without thinking.

"Why?" I asked.

"Why should you ask?" she said, turning toward her house. David followed her like a dog on a short leash while I stood there still wet to the bone with my golden sword.

"What about Lisa?" I yelled to David.

"What about her?"

"I'll see you later, David," I called back. He turned around with a huge smile on his face and waved.

As I watched them walk into the house, I was

thinking of Dottie and her purple coat she had on and wondered if she'd have the same coat on the next time I see her. Then I thought about David with his wet waders on and the awful smell from Sewer Lane.

"I hope he still gets it," I said to myself.

I walked home and slipped my sword out and hid it in the bushes next to the house. When I took off my wet waders and turned them around to dump the water out, I saw a small piece of glass fall on the ground. I picked up the piece and realized it was a small cut diamond.

"Where the hell did--?" I dropped my waders to the ground pulled the sword out from the bushes. The handle of the sword was filled with small diamonds that I hadn't noticed before. "Wow," I whispered, when suddenly the front door opened. I quickly tossed the sword back into the bushes and slid the diamond into my pocket.

"You're not coming into the house until you strip down!" my mother said. "And after you take a shower and get dressed, call Whitney. She's been calling all morning looking for you. She said it was important."

28

"Whitney, what's up?" I asked, acting like nothing was going on even though I heard from the neighborhood crier that the police visited her house earlier.

"My mother just came home from the jail," she said in a low tone. "Can I come up?" I paused for a long while. "Hello?" she said softly. That voice of hers sounded as innocent, lost.   "Sure, come up. I can't wait to see you," I lied.

When I hung up the phone, I thought about her smile, her imagination, and her soft blue eyes when she looked at me. "I love her in so many ways," I said softly. "Why am I avoiding her?"

I heard someone knocking at the door and ran down the stairs before my mother answered it before me. I swung open the door ready to wrap my arms around that beautiful girl of mine and saw Whitney through the screen door with her face covered in bruises. I looked at her for a moment in awe. I slowly opened the screen door, and stepped back to let her in. I didn't say anything, I didn't have to.

"I was downstairs in the basement getting things ready to show John Parry my art work when Richie came storming in the house, slammed the door and broke the glass. He was shouting for my mom at the top of his lungs, and I heard things crash against the wall. I heard the basement door open, and I saw him walk down the stairs still shouting. He grabbed me by the neck. He pushed me against the wall, screaming that it was my fault they had that big fight, and punched me in the face. He then grabbed me again, threw me against the wall, and then he kicked me in the chest knocking the wind out of me. He destroyed four out of the nine paintings I painted, and then broke my tripod. He ran up the stairs still shouting for mom, and then he left."

I pulled her close and gave her a hug ever so softly. She said she had lain on the cold cement floor for hours trying to regain her breath. She was afraid he had broken one of her ribs. She said she prayed, hoping Richie wouldn't come back and kill her, and then she slowly made it up to the phone, and called the police.

She was in pain, a lot of pain. I listened to her, feeling the small tears running down my cheek. I wanted to kill Richie. I wanted to put a bullet in his head, but the only thing I could do was console her and listen. She slowly reached out and hugged me again. I stood there holding her as long as she wanted me to, and then the phone rang.

My mother walked into the living room holding the new cordless phone, with a disgusted look on her face and handed Whitney the phone.

"Hello," she said, wiping her eyes, and then she hung up the phone. "I have to go." Whitney said and turned around and walked out the door. She looked back at me. "I'll be right back," She said.

"Let me come with you," I shouted.

"No, you stay here. I'll be right back." My mother and I watched her walk down the driveway with her head down.

As usual, my mother was shaking her head. "There is so much trouble down there, Andrew. One of these days that Williams family is not going to have anybody left. They're all going to be dead."

I looked at mom thinking about what she just said. "You're probably right."
David came up the driveway, waving at Whitney, still wearing his wet waders, smiling from ear to ear. He told us the police were down at Whitney's house again and pointed his finger for us to go to the weight room in the basement to talk. My mother wasn't stupid, she knew we weren't going down to work out and shook her head as she walked to the kitchen.

"Yup," David said out loud. "She's great!"

"You knew she wanted you, didn't you?" I watched David pacing back and forth, excited as though he won the lottery. Did he?

"Wow, man, she was like—she was so—" He was speechless. He obviously had forgotten that he had a girlfriend. But I didn't remind him. I let him have that moment of happiness.

"So, give me some details. I want some details," I said. Like does she have nice boobs?

"Awe man, she was like so—when she took her shirt off, she took my hands and—wow, nothing like that has ever happened to me before. Then she kissed me and—man, I don't know what to say. Dude, she was, she was just great." I smiled, catching the slight imagination he gave me, but still, does she have nice boobs?

"Whitney is on the phone!" my mother yelled from the top of the stairs.

For the first time I could recall, David looked at me with total disappointment.

"What?" I asked, thinking he was going to say something derogatory toward Whitney. "Nothing," he said.

I stomped up the stairs knowing what he was thinking about in some sort of a strange way, but I also wondered what he wanted to say. I picked up the phone and heard Whitney and her mother speaking to each other in an argumentative tone of voice. "Hello," I said loudly.

"Hey," Whitney said quickly. "Can I come back up?"

"Sure," I answered her, wondering why she even called in the first place. The phone went dead. I looked at my mother staring at me from the living room as I hung up the phone.

"I'm out of here," David said, and pulled open

Andrew LeBel

the door. "Call you later."

Whitney never showed up at the door. I waited all day.

29

David and I jumped out of Jonathan's beat up truck across the street from Roger's Funeral Home. The home was built to look like an eighteenth-century colonial with picture-perfect gardens and lawns, and yet really was only a few years old.

Jonathan looked at me with bloodshot eyes. He was dressed in a suit that looked like it had never been worn. He hesitated as he shut the door of the truck, then stepped off the curb and crossed the street. Jay was his closest friend. Jay was a popular kid. Jay was a Pentucket football star. Jay was just too young to die.

I looked back at him, and my eyes started to well up. I wiped them dry before Jonathan could see. David didn't wait for us. He walked across the street with his head down. Sergeant David Vance was standing tall, directing traffic and wearing a pair of white gloves. He nodded his head without saying anything.

I'd never stepped foot in the funeral home before. I hoped I never would. Sometimes being sixteen you forget that you're mortal, and then the unexpected happens to someone you know. And you never realize that someday it will happen to you. Sooner or later, we all die.

David stepped in the funeral home first, and then Jonathan and I followed. I felt the inevitable eerie cold feeling that I've always imagined, every time I came even remotely close to this place. I saw everyone standing around quietly whispering amongst themselves, and then caught the glimpse of the open casket displayed in the front room just right of the door. Huge bouquets of flowers filled the room. My gut turned upside down. I wanted to puke the minute I saw Jay McClaren lying dead in the Mahogany casket. I stared down at Jay as though I was waiting for him to wake up and yell out "Surprise!" When I heard the news from that piece of shit Luke that Jay McClaren had been killed, I didn't really totally believe him.

Luke told me that Jay had been in a car accident with his brother Scott, and a man named Bob, or something, which was driving too fast. He said Bob lost control of the car and slammed into a tree about a hundred yards from Pentucket High School. Jay was supposed to graduate in the spring, instead he got his head caught under the front seat with his legs slumped over the top. When Luke said Jay's neck was broken, I imagined his head being ripped from his body. When I saw Jay lying in the casket, he looked as though he was just sleeping.

I stared at Jay trying to find any sign

of his injuries, I heard someone behind me saying how good he looks. He's dead, I thought. How can someone look good if they're dead? I felt someone's arm wrap around my waist and pull me tight kissing me on the cheek.

"Thanks for coming," Kristen, Jay's sister, said to me. I noticed her brown eyes were puffy from crying. I wrapped my arm around her, feeling her long, silky, brown hair on my arm and held her tight. She kissed me again on the cheek touching the corner of my lips, and then pulled away from me, looking at her brother one more time before walking into the next room. My eyes followed her until she sat down next to her mother. That was the first time she'd ever kissed me.

"Let's get the hell out of here," Jonathan whispered.

"The service is starting soon. Have a little respect," I told him. David tapped me against the shoulder also looking to leave. I sat down behind Kristen and her family, ignoring him and hoped he'd sit down next to me. Jonathan discreetly flipped me the bird and sat down two chairs away from me. Kristen turned around and looked at me with those big brown eyes of hers and tried to smile. She grabbed my hand, and slightly pulled me forward to sit in the empty chair next to hers. She held onto my hand throughout the service, not even letting go when she needed to pat the tears from her eyes.

Jonathan stood up first after the service and

gave his condolences to the family and squeezed Kristen tight against him for the longest time. David watched him.

"He's such an asshole," he said quietly to me. Kristen's father heard him and coughed.

As Jonathan drove away from the funeral home, I saw Kristen walking down the steps with her mother on her side. She looked up and waved at me watching us until we were out of sight.

Years later, I was walking past a book store, and I saw Kristen's name printed on the front cover of a bestselling mystery novel. I bought the book and opened it before I left the bookstore. It was dedicated to her brother Jay.

I smiled.

30

The night after the funeral, I lay in my bed thinking about Jay McClaren, trying to imagine the last moments of his life. And then I wondered about David, if he was going to wind up dead like Jay. The thought scared me. I considered David to be like a brother and losing him was almost too much to bear.

"Hey!" I heard someone call out, and I head footsteps coming up the stairs. It was Dottie, and she was wearing her curvy purple coat.

"Hey Dottie," I said surprised. She was been the last person I expected to see in my house. "What are you doing here?" I sat up on my bed looking at the cluttered mess around my room, feeling a little embarrassed.

"Nothing, just thought I'd come over and say hi," She sat down on my bed next to me. Her perfume smelled nice, sexy, romantic.

I swiped my hands down my jeans, wiping away the nervous sweat from my palms. I didn't have a clue of why she was here, but I liked having her sitting next to me. She smiled at me and looked at my desk. She walked over and picked up some of my writing material and read a couple lines.

"Nice work. Are you writing a book?" she asked, putting the papers back down out of the order they were in.

"Trying to, anyway," I answered

"What are you writing about?" she asked as she unbuttoned the four big black buttons of her purple coat. I watched every move she made. She smiled wider as she slowly slid her coat off her shoulders. She wore a white soft furry shirt that hung off her shoulders. Her neck was elegantly wrapped in a V-shaped, tri-colored gold necklace. She dropped her coat to her hands and tossed it on the spare bed. She slowly pulled the hair clip from her hair, letting it drop around her shoulders.

"Jesus," I whispered softly. She was more beautiful than I imagined. She was more beautiful than Whitney.

"Us," I said. She looked at me funny not understanding. "I mean, I'm writing about the neighborhood and some of the things that have happened."

"Oh," she said, sounding uninterested. She looked out the window forcing her hands deep in her back pockets as her jeans slid down off her waist and showing the top of her asset. I wanted to wrap my arms around her, touch the softness of her curvy body, and hold her tight against me. She looked at me with a half smile, as the sun reflected off her necklace. "Hell," I said out loud, and walked over, and did what I wanted to do.

She closed her eyes when I slid my hands under her shirt. Her skin was warm to the touch and as soft as silk. My body trembled with excitement. I wanted her bad. I wanted her more than Whitney. Dottie leaned her head back when I touched her breasts covered with a lace bra. I kissed her ever so lightly on the neck gently squeezing her breasts. She pulled her hands from her pockets and slowly turned around. She kissed me on the lips and slid her hands under my shirt. Her hands were cold, but nice. She kissed me again with her tongue touching my lower lip and looked at me as she lowered my hands from her shirt.

"I have to go," she whispered.

"Why?" I asked. She didn't say anything to me. She just picked up her purple coat and quietly left, leaving me hanging with wishful thoughts quickly deteriorating in my head and an arousal that had tightened my pants. Lust was replaced by anger. I gritted my teeth. I hated her for leaving me excited like this. I wanted to punch the window out I was so mad. I heard laughter coming from downstairs and walked to the top of the steps and looked down. I saw David, Dottie, Ditz, and my older sister all looking up at me.

"Hey!" David shouted. "Come down here!" I walked down the stairs still listening to the laughter. Dottie reached out and gave me a hug and kiss, and then they all shouted simultaneously, "April Fools' Day!"

"Assholes," I said, my face burning. But I

couldn't help but smile. Dottie hugged me again tight and whispered in my ear. "We gotcha, and someday I will get you. I liked the way your hands felt on me."

"I can't wait." I said. "I hate you guys." I loved them all.

31

I walked down to Whitney's house after supper to see if I could ask her to give me some of her paintings to show John Parry her work. When I turned the corner near the smashed in mailboxes, I saw John's light blue custom van parked in her driveway.

"Good," I said out loud. I walked up to the door, the window still broken from Richie's temper tantrum and knocked loud enough for the whole neighborhood to hear. Whitney's brother opened the door.

"She's busy right now, puss bag, so I suggest you come back some other year." He shut the door before I had a chance to speak.

"You're such an asshole!" I shouted and walked away pissed off. If it weren't for me, she would have never had John come see her paintings. I looked up at her window, hoping I could see her, and then remembered she would likely be down in the basement with John Parry.

As I walked up the hill toward home, I heard Jonathan's loud truck rumbling up the hill. I stepped onto the sidewalk to avoid getting hit, and then heard his tires squeal to a halt. He rolled down the window, pulled out the cigarette he had behind his ear, and stuck it into his mouth. I saw the Tweedle's sitting next to him. I'm sure Jonathan forced them to be with him in some black-mail-ish way. He probably told them he was going to throw them in the river from the Rocks Village Bridge if they didn't come along for the ride.

"What's going on?" he asked.

"Nothing, just bored," I said. "No one's around." Dottie looked at me with a smile, then secretly blew me a kiss. I remembered the April Fools' joke and wondered when the day was going to be when she was going to, as she said, get me.

"I have some beers. We're going to the pits and hang out. You want to come?" he pulled the lighter from his dashboard and lit his cigarette puffing out a cloud of smoke.

"Wow," I thought to myself. Jonathan is asking me to hang out with him. "Okay," I said. Then I wondered if he was going to leave me in there, and I'd have to walk all the way home.

"Hop in," he said.

I jumped at the chance to sit next to Dottie and opened the passenger door. I squeezed next to her feeling her arm wrapping around me with her fingers rubbing my shoulder. She smelled good. She was wearing her curvy, purple coat. She looked sexy. Jonathan burned rubber as we passed Whitney's house

"Dude, she's fuckin' bad news, man," Jonathan said. Dotz and Ditz looked at me, nodding their heads in agreement. I wanted to defend her and tell them she was a great girl, and that she was just going through hard times. But I couldn't say a word.

When Jonathan tossed the truck into four wheel drive, he slowly drove over the pile of dirt that was supposed to prevent anybody from entering the pits. I began thinking about Whitney. I began to think maybe Jonathan was right, she was bad news.

Just as Jonathan stopped the truck near the huge fire pit and jumped out, Dottie kissed me hard on the lips as fast as she could without Jonathan seeing.

"Wow," I said and smiled at her. I opened the door and almost fell on my face, since the bastard parked the truck over a ditch. Jonathan threw a beer my way and cracked one open for himself. Both Ditz and Dotz sat on the log next to each other with a large bottle of Jack Daniel's Ditz was hiding in her coat. I chugged the beer down without coming up for air and crushed it into a saucer tossing it into the back of his truck. Jonathan was nice enough to throw me another one.

"She's bad news, dude," Jonathan said again. I looked at him wanting to flip him the bird, but Dottie was looking at me in a disappointed way, and I got the urge to run over to her and kiss her. I didn't argue with him, I just nodded my head. Then I heard something from Jonathan I never thought to hear in a million years.

"You know, Dottie has eyes for you. Why don't you take her?" I accidentally dropped my beer in the sand. Luckily for me it landed standing up without losing a single drop. Dottie looked at me with a big smile from ear to ear, nodding her head. I was in shock. Jonathan was giving me a piece of his harem. The world must be coming to an end.

"Are you feeling okay, Jonathan?" I asked. "How many beers have you had already?"

"Dude, I'm just saying, I think you should find someone else to push." We all knew what he meant by the word push. Dottie and Deanna especially didn't like that phrase because Jonathan's definition of push, is getting laid. It made the girls feel cheap.

The sound of a exhaust echoed the sandpit, and a huge, black Chevy Blazer with big tires crawled around the large sand pile. Randy Grasso, a kid with a mullet we all knew and most of us liked. He was kind of a quiet kid who had an amazing resemblance to Sylvester Stallone, except for a scraggly goatee hanging off his chin. Randy's father, back in his heyday, was a middle-weight champion boxer in Europe. His title was Sebastian "Babe" Grasso. I remembered sitting in the living room with pictures of Randy skiing, and his three much older sisters sitting pretty in their class pictures tacked to the wall. Zeb, as Randy called his dad, would occasionally tell us in detail some of his stories of all his wins, and no losses. He bragged about being undefeated. I listened with interest but sometimes wondered if any of it was actually true. Randy always sat next to his dad, rolling his eyes looking bored. I had to try my hardest not to laugh.

Next to the table lamp, there was a black and white picture of Babe in his white shorts. His hands were fisted tight in boxing gloves, and he had a determined look on his face. He stood tall, was broad shouldered and strong. His hands looked powerful enough to smash through a concrete wall. Intimidating as the picture was, Babe Grasso was a gentle soul who cared about his family and everything around him. He was most proud of his only son.

Deanna rolled her eyes and leaned her head against Dottie's shoulder quietly swearing in her ear. She was Randy's ex-girlfriend from last summer. Randy had this thing one night with this chunky looking blonde chick he met at a Fourth of July party. Deanna caught them "pushing" in his blazer. Randy denied it, but Deanna never forgave him and never spoke to him again.

Randy stopped his truck next to Jonathan's and jumped out wearing his beat up cowboy boots. He looked into my eyes with his big baby blues.

"Nose," he said my nickname that nobody ever says but him in a sarcastic tone, and walked over to Jonathan holding his hand out for a beer. Apparently Jonathan must have called him and invited him along.

"What are you up to, Randy?" I asked. He looked at me cracking his beer open, then looked at the Tweedle's like he wanted to say something mean, but he just glanced at me again blowing the foam off the top.

"Drinking," he said.

"As usual, a man of many words," I said.

Deanna stood up and walked toward the trail that led to the deep water hole. Randy watched her in silence, sipping his beer rather delicately. I could tell he wanted to mend the relationship with her, but he was the type of person who never came right out and tried to make things better. He would rather just leave things alone.

Dottie looked at me and winked. "You coming?" she asked me quietly. I wanted to drop everything and go wherever she wanted to go, but I just sat there on the log without saying a word, staring into her beautiful eyes and remembering the feel of her lace bra.

"Whitney is not the girl for you," she said, walking toward Deanna. I cringed when she said that. I hated her for saying that. "Damn you!" I shouted. Jonathan and Randy stopped talking and looked at me.

"Problem?" Randy questioned.

"No," I said and took another swig of my beer. I crushed the empty can against my head.

"Have another beer," Jonathan said and tossed me a third. "She's bad news, dude," Jonathan said for the third time.

"Whitney," Randy said with a smirk. "She's someone I wouldn't touch. She probably has V.D." I looked at him, ready to throw a rock and hit him between the eyes, but the only thing I did do was leave. I walked away heading toward the water hole where the girls were. I stopped dead in my tracks a short distance from them. Their clothes were neatly folded on the ground, and both were swimming in the icy water.

I quietly went back to the fire pit, just as Randy jumped into his truck. I wondered where he was going when all the beer is right here.

32

Tweedle Dotz came up the trail alone, holding her arms across her chest. She sat down next to me, her hair dripping wet. She smiled at me and took a huge swig from her bottle of Jack. Her clothes were stuck to her body like a wet newspaper.

"Did you like our little surprise?" she asked, wiping her mouth.

"What surprise?"

"Whew, that was refreshing." Ditz said plumping down next to Dotz, bumped her shoulder, and pulled the bottle from her hand. Jonathan stared at them as he finished his second beer and reached into grab another.

"You girls at it again?" he asked with a slight giggle. Dotz smiled at me, and then quickly stuck her middle finger up high in the air at him.

"They weren't doing anything," I said. I looked at Dotz and Ditz, wondering if Jonathan knew a lot more than I about what they did or did not do.

"Have another beer, drunk," he said, tossing another beer my way, making it my sixth or was it my fifth? I had lost track. Dottie kissed me on the lips and slid her tongue in my mouth. I became aroused touching her soft lips, feeling her tongue slide across mine and smelling her sexy perfume somewhat diluted from the water but still noticeable. I backed away when I heard Randy's Blazer rumbling around the sand pile.

"Where did Randy go?" I asked, putting the beer between my legs.

"He'll be back, drunk, don't worry," Jonathan said laughing. Ditz suddenly jumped on the other side of me and slid her hand under my shirt. I tightened up from her cold hands on my back. She laughed affectionately. Dottie followed suit, putting her cold hands under my shirt against my chest. Suddenly it dawned on me when I saw Jonathan staring at us like he was watching a porn movie. It was a trick. But feeling the girls' hands on me, I didn't care.

Randy's blazer pulled into the pits. Another person was sitting in the passenger seat. The sun was slowly setting beyond the trees, making it hard to see who was in the blazer with him. The girls' hands felt good, nice, and smooth. I was embracing the moment. I was in heaven feeling the small circles Dottie was making, and the small kisses Deanna was giving. I saw the person jump out of Randy's big blazer and walked toward the fire pit.

Whitney.

"Shit."

33

I heard through the neighborhood grape-vine a couple days later that John Parry took some of Whitney's paintings to someone he knew in Maine to see if they would display them in their galley. When I heard that, I smiled. I was proud of Whitney. I wanted to congratulate her, but after the setup my so-called friends put me through, I'd rather shoot myself in the foot then deal with that bullshit again.

She said she never wanted to see me again. She told me, screaming at the top of her lungs if I so much even thought about knocking on her door, she was going to take her mother's gun and shoot me in the head like her dog. What a bad night, but I did have a great time with the Twee-dles

David came up the stairs wearing his waders and slammed his ass down on the top step. I looked at him wondering why he had his ice floating attire on since it's been in the sixties all week.

"What are you doing?" I asked him, lying on my bed.

"What's your problem?".

"Whitney dumped me like a sack of shit," I said.

"Yeah so"

"What the fuck!" I shouted in anger.

"Get your shit on, and let's go, dumbass."

"Where,"

"Its tunnel running season," he said. I jumped off my bed, being excited and put on my gear. Three years ago we went tunneling and found a black suitcase next to the highway. We hesitated for days to open it, thinking we found some buried treasure, and thought about how we were going to spend the money. In the end we opened it up, and all that was in the suitcase was dirty clothes.

We ran under the highway tunnels once the ice had melted hoping for that lost treasure, that suitcase full of cash. It was really just another way for us to be kids a little while longer.

We made it down to the highway talking about the girls we "pushed" and who we'd like to. I noticed the air was a lot colder than it had been, and it felt like snow was coming. David stepped into the longest tunnel that went under the south bound side of the highway. We imagined the tunnel was the secret entrance-way to the Locust Street Cemetery because it was so dark, and we were afraid someday we were going to step on a dead body. As we walked through the tunnel, the smell of an animal got stronger with every step, we heard the sound of the cars passing over head.

We hopped from side to side trying not to step into the stream under our feet, when suddenly we heard a snap that sounded like a branch breaking. We stopped dead in our tracks in the pitch black of the tunnel.

"What the hell was that?" I asked.

"I don't know," David answered. "Where's your lighter, David?"

"I got it," he said reaching into his waders and flicked the lighter.

"Oh shit!" he shouted. I came closer and bent down to get a closer look.

"Oh shit!" I shouted. "What the hell?"

"It's a skeleton of a dog!" David said.

"No shit! Where'd you get that idea?" I said sarcastically. David dropped the lighter in the water after it burned his finger. I turned around and hobbled back to the opening. The entrance looked so close, and yet it took us a long time to get there. When we reached it, it was snowing hard. We managed to jump the railing onto the road just as Whitney's Bigfoot brother drove by us at a snail's pace. I watched for a moment watching him step on the brakes every so often. "Here comes the fuzz," David said.

"Great, what do you want to do?"

"Let's see who it is first." The cruiser drove by without even looking at us, and neither of us recognized the cop.

We walked back to the bridge in silence, jumped the guard rail sliding down the hill on the other side of the road, and then shuffled along the dark tunnel that headed toward Amesbury.

"Hey!" We heard a girl's voice shout from the opening. She was too far away to make out who she was, but I recognized the voice. The way my gut started feeling, I knew it wasn't going to be good.

34

"It's Whitney," I whispered. "Shit. What the hell does she want?

"Maybe she wants to make up."

"Yeah, with a bullet hole in my head"

"Don't think so," David said.

"What are you doing here?" I yelled.

"I want to talk to you!" she shouted.

"She wants to kill me," I whispered to David. He started to laugh as we walked toward her.

"How did you know we were here?" I shouted.

"Jimmy told me!"

"Oh, her brother the Bigfoot," I stopped about twenty feet away, expecting her to pull out her mother's gun and shoot me right between my eyes. David pushed me to keep moving, but the thought of dying in the tunnel didn't sit in my stomach very well. "Hey, Whit, what's going on?" David asked, still pushing me along.

"Cheater said to say hi if I saw you. So, hi from her," Whitney said to him. David smiled. He had told me he called her a couple of times, and each time someone else from our school answered the phone. I told him to forget about her. Remember,

I kept saying, she's "Cheater." He soon realized she was just doing what she does best. He went back to looking through the window of Donna's house again, hoping to get a glimpse of her boobs.

"What are you doing here, Whit?" I asked again nervously, watching every move she made.

"I wanted to apologize for what I said at the pits. Jonathan told me about the little joke everyone played on you. He said he didn't think I was going to get that upset. He told me it was just a joke among friends."

"Jonathan is not my friend," I said, gritting my teeth. "He's an asshole."

"Then why did you go to the pits with him?" I didn't have a good reason. The only thing I thought about was Dottie. That made me smile, and Whitney seemed to read my mind. Her eyes bore into mine accusingly, and her hands were clenched at her sides.

"I went with them because Jonathan asked me if I wanted to go drinking, and I knew Randy was going to be there," I said, praying she'd believe that lie. Whitney took a deep breath and relaxed her hands still staring at me with daggers.

"You didn't go because of one of the girls there, did you?" she asked.

"No, why would I do something like that?"

"Jonathan wouldn't give up one of his bitches, Whit," David blurted out, saving my ass. "He gets mad if someone even so much as looks at them in the hall at school."

Whitney seemed to consider that for a moment and stared deep into my eyes. Finally, she relaxed and wrapped her arms around me, kissing me on the cheek. I squeezed her hesitantly, and felt her breasts against me. I closed my eyes remembering the day she came to my house, and we just laid there on my bed holding each other. I kissed her gently on the neck as her perfume started to tingle my nose. I fell in love with her all over again. I wanted to go home with her.

"Get a room!" David shouted.

"I'm going home," Whitney said, looking at me as though she wanted me to follow. I wanted to go in the worst way and make up for the time we lost. I wanted to hear all about the visit with John Richard Parry. I wanted it all. I looked at David thinking maybe we needed to go too, but the look on David's face made it clear that he expected me to stay with him.

"I'll come down later," I said. "David and I have some things we need to do today."

"I'll be home down in the basement waiting." She kissed me, sliding her hand across my face. I watched her turn away and slowly crawl up the hill to the road. I waved one more time before I walked back into the tunnel, but she didn't look back at me. I thought about her the whole time David and I ran under the highway. I'm sure David knew I wanted to be with her, but tunnel running was a tradition we'd upheld since we were six years old, and I think he was determined that nothing was going to ruin it.

We managed to hold the tradition for six more years, and not once did we ever run through the longest tunnel, hoping to find out if the other side was the secret entrance to Locust Street Cemetery. It was just too damn scary. We never found anything worth keeping either.

35

I knocked on Whitney's door that night after supper, expecting to see Bigfoot Jimmy. What I didn't expect to see was Whitney's mom crying again. She opened the door wider and walked away without saying anything. When I walked into the house, there were a lot of papers scattered on the floor. I picked one of them up out of curiosity. It read: District Court State of Massachusetts, verses Barbara Williams. I threw it back on the floor before I read anything else and quietly walked down the basement stairs.

I saw Whitney standing in front of a brand new tripod her brother had bought her after Richie decided to break the other one. Surprisingly enough, I saw Cheater sitting on the stool next to her, wearing her usual wife beater tanktop, and nothing much else.

"What are you doing?" I asked, thinking Whitney was going to drop everything, and give me a hug. Instead she just looked at me from the corner of her eye, still painting her picture. Cheater waved at me lightly and wore an unusual stiff looking smile. I glanced at the canvas and realized Whitney was painting Cheater's portrait. "Wow," I said, looking at Cheater's chest. Her semi see-through T-shirt drew my attention. *They're so big!* I thought. She winked at me with a flirtatious smile, knowing I wasn't looking at the painting

"What did John Parry have to say about your work?" I asked, prying my attention away from the model and back to Whitney.

"He liked my work, but he also said I needed to be more creative other than just making pictures of simpleness."

"What's that suppose to mean?"

"It means I need to be a better painter!" she snapped at me and slapped the paint brush against the canvas, smudging Cheaters cheek. On that note, I left without saying anything else.

I made it to the bashed in mailboxes when I heard my name being called. I saw Cheater coming out of Whitney's house putting her coat on. "Now what?" I said out loud, rolling my eyes. Cheater called to me again, waving her arm around like she was flagging down a New York taxi. I waited for her to see exactly what she wanted.

"What are you doing?" she asked, running up to me, somewhat out of breath.

"What is there to do other than freeze my ass off?" I answered her. She looked over her shoulder at Whitney's house. I wondered if she had something on her mind, and she didn't want Whitney to know.

"Do you want to hang out?" she asked, taking my hand. I stared at her briefly, remembering when she said the same thing a couple days ago, and David ended up losing his virginity.

"What about Whitney?" I asked.

"I'm done hanging out with her, and besides, she said she wanted to finish my painting without me." I looked at Cheater's house with the snow just over the bottom window sill, and her bedroom window where she stared out at the world as though she were waiting for something that would never come.

"Okay," I said.

Cheater opened the door and stepped in, still holding my hand nice and tight.

"Take off your coat." She told me, taking her own coat off. I looked at her and instantly thought about all the wrong thoughts

"Meredith," I said.

"What," she answered with a tone of voice that made it clear if I left, she'd be pissed.

"Nothing," I said. *I'm in trouble*, I thought putting my coat on a wooden chair.

"Let's go upstairs," she said grabbing my hand again. Every time I stepped up on the staircase heading to her room, I felt like I was making each step closer to my grave if Whitney found out what I was doing. Even though Whitney considered Meredith to be her best friend until Peter raped her. She didn't trust her as far as she could throw her after that. I didn't blame her, and now she had me trapped in her web. Meredith opened her bedroom door, still holding my hand and walked in.

"I'm gonna take these jeans off, they feel too tight," she said, pulling her green sweats out of her bureau. I looked around her white-walled bedroom with all the centerfold pictures of naked men, tanned bodies, and frontal views. I felt the urge to run out as fast as I could, until I turned around, and saw Cheater standing in her bathroom wearing just her green bikini underwear. I stared at her with amazement. I couldn't take my eyes off of her. She stood there in front of the mirror brushing her hair with the door wide open, as though I wasn't here. Suddenly, she looked at me, and I spun my head in another direction almost giving myself whiplash. Meredith walked out of the bathroom, wrapped her arms around me, and kissed me on the lips. I instantly felt uncomfortable but excited at the same time and wrapped my arms around her bare body sliding my hands under her underwear.

Whitney is going to kill me, I thought. But I didn't care.

36

Guilty as sin I was. I didn't want the girl of my dreams to ever find out I had the exotic pleasure of spending the day with her best friend, naked. David called the next morning, and the same monotone voice came over the phone line.

"I'll be down." I hung up the phone and looked out the window for David. It was cold outside, very cold. It had snowed for two days since we went tunnel running, and both of us knew Sewer Lane was going to be frozen again. But when I saw David come up the driveway, I noticed he didn't have his waders on.

"Hey," he said.

"What's going on?" I asked him.

"Nothing, Luke got busted again yesterday," he told me. I stared into his eyes. I wanted to jump up and yell hooray, but I kept cool. "What for this time?" I asked.   "Breaking and entering some old bitch's house last night around ten o' clock. The old lady said they attacked her and sexually assaulted her."

"No shit." I couldn't help thinking Luke wouldn't stoop down that low.

"What do you want to do?" David asked, changing the subject.

"I thought maybe we would go down to Sewer Lane, but I see you don't have your waders on."

"Dad's using them today. He went ice fishing with a friend of his at the lake. Let's just go walk around."

We walked down the street in silence, feeling the face-cracking cold, passing the smashed in mailboxes. David looked at me as though he had something else on his mind. He leaned against the telephone pole and popped the last spearmint candy he had left in his pocket into his mouth, tossing the clear wrapper into the wind.

"What?" I asked, wondering what the hell his problem was.

"I got to tell you something." I stared at him, already thinking whatever he's got to spill his guts with, it's not going to be good.

"Roger Cass is out of jail. He told one of Luke's friends he's going to kill Whitney as soon as he gets his hands on her." My heart stopped.

"Oh shit!" I yelled out loud. "What the hell? How the hell did he get out of jail?"

"I don't know, maybe his mom bailed him out."

"We have to do something." I was frantic. I was scared for Whitney.

We walked further down the street stopping in front of Whitney's house. I looked up at her window, and saw her sitting at her white desk, fixing her hair. I knocked on the door waiting for her Bigfoot brother to tell me to take a hike, and then the door opened with her mother smiling at me.

"Whitney's upstairs," she said and as usual, she walked away leaving me to shut the door. I stepped in the house, smelling an awful smell as though someone had died in the bathroom. David stayed on the old porch.

"I'm going to Luke's and find out what happened," he told me. I didn't say anything, I just watched him leave. "I'll come down later!" I yelled. He didn't answer. He didn't turn around. He was mad.

I slowly walked up the stairs as quietly as I could and walked along the wall so the hardwood floor wouldn't creek and betray my presence. I looked into Whitney's room and saw her standing at her white desk looking into the mirror. She looked beautiful, sexy. Impure thoughts came to mind. She wore a short white lace night gown, with her hair reaching to the middle of her back. I admired her through the doorway like a peeping tom in the window, and then I stepped into her room letting her see me in the mirror behind her. She quickly turned her head, and smiled as wide as she could. "Hey, Whit," I said.

"What are you doing here?" she asked. I watched her turn around, and stand in the sunlight shining through the window. I could see her naked body through her night gown. I walked closer to her, taking off my coat, when suddenly I felt a vise grip against my shoulder, pushing me to the floor.

37

I looked up and saw her stupid Bigfoot brother standing tall over me with an "I'm gonna beat you senseless" look on his face.

"Jimmy, what are you doing?" Whitney yelled. Jimmy looked at her gritting his teeth. I honestly could say I really hated her brother more than Roger Cass. I couldn't wait until the glorious day came when Whitney said her brother went back to Alaska. Let the bastard freeze his ass off.

"This asshole friend of yours has some bad news to tell you! Don't you, cowboy!" he shouted gripping my shoulder even harder. The pain became excruciating to the point my eyes filled up with tears.

"Jimmy, you're hurting him! Stop it!"

"Not until he says the bad news!"

"Aaahh," I screamed, twisting my body closer to the floor. "Let me go!"

"Say it, asshole!"

"Jimmy, stop!" Whitney's mother yelled. Just as I was going to tell Whitney about Roger, Whitney's mother grabbed Jimmy's arm, and slapped him across the face. "We already know the Cass boy is out, so let go of his shoulder." Jimmy released his vise grip at the same time pushed me harder to the floor. The pulsating pain still throbbed as I felt like my shoulder was ripped in half. "Roger Cass is home?" Whitney asked. The terror in her eyes was clear. I got up off the floor, rubbing my shoulder. Jimmy looked at me one more time before he went down the stairs. "Mom," Whitney whispered. The tension was so thick, it could have smothered me.

Whitney's mom didn't say anything; she just looked at her in disappointment, nodded her head, and walked away.

"I wouldn't worry too much about Roger," I lied. I didn't have a clue of what was going to happen in the future, but it sounded good.

Whitney paced back and forth across the floor, passing the window, revealing her naked body underneath. I didn't care about Roger and his deadly motives. I cared about seeing Whitney. I cranked my arm around trying to ease the pain, but it didn't help.

"Come here and give me a hug," I said. Whitney stopped and looked at me. She hesitantly came to me, wrapped her arms around me and put her head down on the shoulder her brother just got done twisting. I could feel her silently crying and shivering with fear. She was scared. She was terrified. I held her for a long time feeling my clothes beginning to stick to my skin, and I slowly pushed her away. I kissed her on the lips and looked into her eyes. I knew what I needed to do. I needed to save Whitney from sure death. I needed to save my girl's life from the devil. I needed to kill Roger Cass.

38

The next morning, I went downstairs thinking about that piece of shit Roger Cass. I was heading for the bathroom, when I saw the golden sword lying on the kitchen table. I froze, my heart stopped; I was going to die today. I went into the bathroom listening for every move, every slight little sound. Next to the phone hung a paddle with the word WHACK printed on it. John Parry had made it years earlier and donated it to the church rummage sale. My mother had bought it. She said she hung it up to remind me to be a good boy. Luckily for me she had never used it. But that was bound to change now.

I opened the bathroom door ever so slowly and peaked around the corner. I saw my mother with her arms crossed leaning against the kitchen counter, holding the paddle. "Oh shit," I whispered to myself. I walked out of the bathroom with my head down, waiting for the pain.

"Where the hell did you get this thing?" she asked, gritting her teeth and lightly tapping the paddle against the counter.

"I found it," I lied. My mother stared at me

with fire in her eyes.

"You stole it," she whispered. "You stole it from that old boarded up house across the river. Didn't you?" I became very scared. I looked at the paddle when my mother dropped her arms and stepped forward. She was going to break the paddle over my ass. It was going to really hurt.

"Tell me where you stole this from, or I swear you won't sit down for a week." She gripped the paddle hard enough her knuckles turned white. Suddenly the phone rang. I grabbed the phone and pressed it to my ear before my mother could stop me..

"Hey," David said on the other end. "I'll be down." I didn't say anything; I just hung up the phone.

"That was David, wasn't it?" my mother asked. I nodded my head staring down at the paddle.

"He's coming down?" she asked. I nodded my head again. "Good," she said. "Maybe he can tell me the truth since you won't." I stood in the kitchen waiting for David in silence with my mother ready to pounce on me like a hungry wolf eyeing a rabbit when the door slid open.

"David," my mother said loudly. "Come into the kitchen." David walked in the kitchen with his father's waders on. He saw the sword on the table, and his eyes widened in shock. He looked at me, and then saw my mother holding the whack paddle.

"Oh, shit," he whispered.

"Tell me, David, where did this sword come from?" David looked at me squirming around in his waders looking for a good lie, but the only thing he said was. "I don't know." I was dead. My mother twisted the paddle around in her hand like a samurai warrior. David took a deep breath and relaxed his body against the dryer.

"Me and Andy got it from the old haunted house across the river a couple weeks ago." My mother stopped twisting the paddle around and dropped it next to the sword. David looked at me, hoping he put us in the clear by telling the truth. It didn't.

"I'm not going to do anything right now," she said. "But this situation is not over."

"Mom, I'm sorry," I said. "I didn't think I was stealing it if no one lived in the house." My mother handed me the paddle and told me to hang it up. I took it from her, feeling the sweat on my palm and almost dropped it on the floor. My mother shook her head, grabbed the sword off the table, and slid the blade out of its sheath. I was in awe of the beautiful shine of the smooth cold steel. I wanted to reach for the sword and hold it in my hand like a gold digger finding his first nugget. Then my mother slid the sword back in the sheath, and I heard a loud click as though she locked it. She laid the sword down on the table and looked at both of us in disgust.

"I don't care what you do with this sword.

I don't care where you put it but don't ever let me see it in this house again." I reached for the sword, but my mother swung around and looked at me fiercely.

"I was talking to David. You can go upstairs to your room until I say you can come out." I dropped my hand and walked with my head down. I didn't look at David, I just went upstairs and lay down on my bed. I listened to every movement downstairs, listening for the scrape of the sword off the table. I heard nothing but the door opening and shutting as David left holding the sword.

I heard my mother walk up the stairs, and she opened the door and looked at me with disgust.

"I never thought I'd see the day when you started acting just like your son-of-a-bitch father," she said. I felt a tear run down the side of my face. I didn't say anything; I didn't have anything to say.

The next day, I heard my mother getting ready to leave to go to work. I played sick hoping my mother would let me stay home from school, and just before she said anything, I ran into the bathroom with my fingers jammed down my throat, heaving until I puked. It worked. I stayed home. I went down into the cellar and scouted around for a hammer and nail. I ran up the stairs holding that hammer and stared at that damn WHACK paddle. I carefully placed the nail on the paddle and nailed the bastard to the wall.

39

Late at night, somewhere around 11:30pm on a Wednesday, Roger Cass stared at Whitney's house from across the road. He looked through the dark windows for any movement. He remembered which bedroom window was Whitney's on the second floor. "She's such a bitch, and she deserves to die," he whispered and saw his breath swirling in the cold air. He stuck his hands deep into his coat pockets, wondering how he was gonna get Whitney. He wanted to kill her. He wanted to get revenge for his own brother's death. His mother told him, time and time again: "Make sure we get even with that disgusting Williams family. Kill that bitch if you have to. Peter's dead because of her."

Roger walked closer with his steel-toed work boots and leaned his heavy body against the front of Whitney's dead father's Mercedes, that was just barely parked in the driveway. He thought about just rushing in the house, and bashing Whitney in the head with a metal pipe. He didn't know what to do, but he wanted to please his mother. She was his life. She was his only reason he was still alive.

He remembered long ago, he was playing around the river's edge with his brother and slipped off the rocks into the water. The current was strong. Strong enough, it quickly took him down the river, as he screamed for help. His mother dove into the water, grabbed him by the hair, and pulled him ashore. He always remembered his mother saved his life that day, and he never could, or will ever forget it.

Roger pulled a cigarette out from his coat pocket, and then sparked up his lighter. He heard a noise just before he could suck in the cigarette smoke and felt a sharp object piercing through the center of his back, the point coming through the front of his coat before being pulled out. "What the..." he said, dropping the cigarette onto the driveway. Roger turned around and saw a woman, her face covered with a black knitted winter hat, holding a long golden sword. He felt the sword slice across his neck, and watched the blood splatter all over the front of the car. He grabbed his neck feeling the blood drooling through his fingers and fell hard to the ground hard. He dragged himself to the edge of the driveway, and then tried to get to his feet. He felt another stab piercing into his back, and then dropped to the icy pavement.

"Please, please don't kill me," he said, spitting blood as he spoke.

"You will die," he heard a low voice. "You will die." He felt another piercing from the sword in his back. He was weak. His eyes started to roll.

He knew he was dying. He knew his life was over. He turned onto his back, and saw the killer lift her hat off her face, revealing her identity. "You," he whispered and raised his hand up to the woman. Roger felt the sword again slice across his neck. Then all was quiet.

The killer slowly picked up the cigarette from the driveway, took a couple drags, and flicked it far into the snow. She took the golden sword, pointed it against the center of Roger's chest, and pushed it in until the blade hit the pavement. She took a piece of paper out of her pocket and stuck it on the handle of the sword. She then dragged Roger through the snow to the side of the house, and dropped him in the middle of the yard. She smiled knowing her job was finally complete and walked back to the driveway. She was happy. She started whistling as she walked down the road, looking at the icy river from the moonlight.

40

Whitney's brother walked outside in his old smelly bathrobe, first thing in the morning to get the paper that had been thrown into the icy driveway. When he reached down to pick up the paper, he saw dabs of blood scattered all over like shattered glass, and more blood splattered all over the side of the Mercedes. He looked around, holding the paper like a weapon, wondering what, or who was killed. He searched under the car, inside the bushes, thinking maybe it was a stray cat that got hit by a car, and then died somewhere close by. Then he saw a bloody red trail traveling around the house. He stepped into the snow feeling it drop into his slippers with each step. When he rounded the corner, he saw the dead body frozen solid next to the path where the dog trotted back and forth on a leash. He stood next to the body, the dog making whining noises.

"Jesus," he said in a whisper. "Who the ....? Mom!" He screamed loud enough for the whole neighborhood to hear. "Mom!" he screamed again, looking at the dining room window. He saw his mother come to the window holding a hot cup of coffee, and then instantly dropped it to the floor.

Jimmy looked at the corpse again and saw a long golden sword stuck in his chest with a note attached to the top reading, "this is what you wanted, Whitney?" Jimmy lifted the hood over the frozen body and saw that it was Roger Cass covered in blood from head to toe.

"Jesus," he said again in a whisper. "Someone fuckin' beat me to it," Jimmy slapped the paper on his leg, turned around and followed his own foot steps back to the driveway when he started hearing the sirens. When he stepped off the snow and kicked his feet on the driveway, he saw the first of many police cruisers stopping in front of the house.

"This is going to be a long fuckin' day," he said, walking toward the house.

Barbara opened the door, buttoning her coat. She stared at Jimmy with a hundred questions racing through her head. Jimmy squeezed by her in silence, and then went into the living room and sat down. He pulled the paper out of the orange colored plastic bag and snapped it open as though nothing had happened. His mother stood there glaring at him.

"Get up, you friggin' idiot!" she screamed. "Stop acting like you didn't find that dead body out there in the yard!" Jimmy just looked at her and snapped the paper. He didn't want to answer any questions. He didn't want to help. He didn't want to be anywhere close to the cops. He didn't want anyone to know why he moved back from Alaska, especially his own mother.

"I said get up!" Barbara screamed louder.

"Why!" he shouted. "My feet are cold, I don't want to deal with the police, and I just woke up!"

"You need to do something right for a change!"

"Fine, I'll do this just this once. Just remember, I didn't move back from Alaska to deal with some more bullshit. I want to be left alone."

"What do you mean move back?" Barbara questioned. "You never said move back. You said you came to visit for a couple of weeks. What do you mean move back?" There was a knock on the door. "We'll continue with this conversation later." She snapped, and then opened the door and saw Sergeant David Vance standing tall on the old porch in a long dark blue raincoat. "Well, hello, Barbara, you have a dead body in your yard, I hear?"

"Yes, I'll show you where it is." Barbara hurriedly walked into the dining room and pointed to the window. She bent down and picked up the broken mug off the floor, and looked around for a dry cloth that usually hung off a chair. She reached for it and threw it down, and swooshed it around with her foot. Vance saw Jimmy sitting on the couch and swatted the newspaper as he walked by. "It's right there." Barbara said, again pointing out the window. Sgt. Vance looked down at the mess on the floor, and then looked out the window. "Holy Jesus, I guess you do have a dead body in your yard. I'll be right back." He said and headed for the door.

Barbara stared out the window and watched the crowd of police officers swarming around the body. Sgt. Vance had one of the officers tape off the area, and ordered a couple more to stand guard in case some of the neighbors got nosy.

"Who do you suppose that is out there?" Barbara asked, thinking it was probably the old and gray homeless man who always cuts through people's yard, rifling through everyone's trash. "It's Roger Cass, Mom. He got killed by someone who left a note for Whitney stuck to his chest with a sword." Barbara turned around and looked at him with surprise. "What do you mean someone left a note for Whitney? What the hell does Whitney have to do with this?"

"Just what I said, someone left a note with a huge friggin' sword stuck in his chest."

"Great, now the cops will really think Whitney had something to do with it."

"Not me," Jimmy replied. "I had nothing to do with that asshole's murder. Quite frankly, Mom, someone basically beat me to it. I was planning on killing him anyway to help my sister out, but someone else got to him first. What I want to know is, is why did they kill him in our yard?"

"What the hell are you talking about, Jimmy?

181

You're telling me you were going to kill Roger Cass?"

"Look at all the shit Whitney's gone through with that dirt-bag, Mom. We needed to do something, didn't we? He was going to kill her so, why shouldn't we kill him first?"

Sgt. Vance came to the door, knocked twice, and then walked in. He looked right at Jimmy still reading the paper and walked toward Barbara. "Okay, Barbara," he said sternly. He looked at her with his baby blue eyes and smooth clean shaven face. "What the hell happened here last night? That kid out there got mutilated." Barbara saw Jimmy looking at her from the corner of his eye, hoping she would leave him out of it. She wanted to lie and keep Jimmy out of all this mess, but for some strange reason, she came right out and blurted his name. "Jimmy was the one who found the dead body this morning, David. Not me." She took a deep breath, and leaned against the windowsill. Jimmy rolled his eyes pulling the paper closer to hide his face. Sgt. Vance walked over to Jimmy, slammed the paper down, and stared into his eyes. "I've been tired of playing your stupid games since you were twelve, and you know it as well as I do, I've gone through a lot of shit with you. And now you have a dead body out there in your yard, and now you're going to tell me what the fuck happened!" Jimmy dropped the paper from his hand, and looked away.

"I found the stiff this morning when I went out side for the paper." Sgt. Vance wrote down his statement and waited for him to say more.

"I walked around the house and saw him lying in the snow and blood. I lifted his hood to see who the stiff was. That's it, nothing more."

"You have nothing else to add? That's it?"

"Nope, nothing,"

"Why do I get the feeling you're lying to me, as usual."

"David, this time I swear I'm telling the truth. I don't have anything to do with Roger Cass' murder. I swear to fuckin' God."

"What about Whitney?"

"Whitney has nothing to do with it!" Barbara shouted.

"The note stuck to his chest was for her. Let's see," he said, and pulled the note wrapped in plastic from his coat pocket. "This is what you wanted, Whitney?" he read out loud. "So how can you tell me she has nothing to do with the murder, Barbara? Her name is on the note."

"Sgt. Vance, Whitney doesn't have a clue of what's going on right now. She's sleeping for Christ sakes." Sgt. Vance looked at Barbara and slid his pen into his pocket. "Just to let you know, Barbara, we're not going to be leaving anytime soon, so you can start making some god damn coffee for everyone out there because it's friggin' cold outside." Barbara glared at him for a moment, then walked into the kitchen and started the coffee. She looked out the window and saw someone watching from the corner of Mrs. Clancy's house.

41

Barbara saw the woman dressed in army fatigues and a black hat just standing against the house, puffing on a cigarette. "Gee, nothing like telling everyone you're the killer," she said. She turned around and walked to the living room, hoping to catch Sgt. Vance. When she opened the door, she saw a few more police officers talking with Sgt. Vance, but Jimmy was nowhere to be found.

Barbara went upstairs and found Jimmy staring out the bathroom window at the same woman she was looking at downstairs. "Who do you suppose that is?" Barbara asked in a whisper.

"I have no idea, but I would guess it's someone who had a lot to do with Cass's murder."

"Think we should tell the cops?"

"Why? By the time we go down and say something, they'll be long gone."

"Yeah, I suppose you're right." Barbara and Jimmy stood at the window watching the woman as though they were staring at a film. "Is it a man or a woman?" Barbara asked. Jimmy shrugged. Then as they watched for a while the woman turned around and left and disappearing down Friend Street

Sgt. Vance examined the golden sword still stuck in Roger Cass's chest. He pulled the note out of his pocket again and read the handwriting. "Hey, Arty, when is the coroner getting here?" Sgt. Vance asked. Arty looked at Vance with tired eyes. "Well, he should'a been here by now Sarg. Hell, he should'a been here almost an hour go. He's probably still sleepin' wit dat young-in of a wife he has."

"Yeah, you're probably right, Arty."

Jimmy walked outside wondering if the body was still stuck to the ground like a block of ice, when Officer Larsen put his arm out and stopped him before he stepped into the snow.

"Sorry, sir. You can't go over there during an investigation," he said. Jimmy stared at him with hatred. "I was over there before you even showed up, Officer." He said, and then walked back into the house cursing to himself. He slammed the door, went into the dining room, and looked out the window. He saw Roger Cass still dead on the ground with Sgt. Vance kneeling over him, and then from the corner of his eye, he saw the same person dressed in army fatigues across the street sitting on the church steps. "Hey, Mom," he said. "That person we saw standing next to the Clancy's house is sitting on the church steps smoking a butt." Barbara looked out the window and saw the person flick the cigarette butt and light up another. She lightly tapped on the glass to try to get Sgt. Vance's attention when she saw another police officer walking toward the church. "Oh, this oughta be good," Jimmy said. Suddenly, the person got up and quickly walked around the church. "Hey!" the police officer yelled and ran to the other side hoping to catch them. Barbara looked toward the body, took a deep breath, trying to settle her thoughts. She saw an old man carefully stepping through the snow, holding a black leather bag in one hand, and a thick spit wet cigar in the other.

"Jesus," Barbara said. "He looks like the same sick bastard that was at the morgue when Grandma died. Goddamn, it is the same sick bastard. He was the one who was having an affair with his black assistant. I think she was a lot younger than he is."

"That figures," Jimmy said. "People like him should just drown in the Merrimack River like a filthy rat." Jimmy and Barbara stared out the window in silence, watching every move the police made as they packed up Roger Cass in an orange body bag with a thick black zipper and wrapped the golden sword in a black plastic trash bag.

"It's just another day at the Williams's," Barbara said. Jimmy chuckled. Barbara suddenly sniffed the air. "Oh, shit!" she shouted, and ran into the kitchen. She found the tea pot with all the water boiled away, burning the bottom. She shut off the stove, grabbed the handle with a cloth, and tossed it into the sink. "Shit," she said again leaning against the sink. She looked out the window and saw the same person leaning against the Clancy's house again, but this time, she was holding a rifle, pointing it at the house.

42

Barbara watched the person taking aim and heard a pop. The kitchen window cracked and pieces of glass fell into the sink. Barbara fell to her knees. "Jesus! Jimmy!" she shrieked. "Jimmy!" She yelled again. "Someone's shooting at me!" Jimmy came rushing into the kitchen and saw the hole in the window. He looked out and saw the shooter pointing the gun. Pop! More glass fell into the sink. "What the fuck, asshole!" Jimmy shouted through the window. Barbara ran to the dining room and ripped opened the window. "David! Someone's shooting at us!"

"Goddamit, Barbara! Get down! I know someone's shooting at us. I can hear the shots for Christ sakes!" Sgt. Vance looked down and saw the shooter still pointing the gun at the house. He pulled his gun out of his holster and fired three rounds, hitting the Clancy's house, but missing the shooter. The shooter shot one more bullet into the window, and then fled behind the house disappearing. "Go! Go! Go!" Sgt. Vance yelled at his officers.

Barbara went back in the kitchen and saw Jimmy

kneeling on the floor in front of the sink.

"Jimmy, the police went after them.

"I know, Mom, but now you need to take me to the hospital. I've been shot in the shoulder."

Barbara saw all the blood when she lifted his robe away and quickly grabbed a hand towel under the sink, placing it on the wound. She forced her voice to be calm. "Come on Jimmy. Let's go. Can you make it to the car?"

"Yeah, I'll be okay, I can walk," he said. "I just need to stop bleeding."

"Barbara!" Sgt, Vance shouted from the front door.

"We're in here! Jimmy's been shot!" Sgt. Vance hurried into the kitchen and grabbed a hold of Jimmy and helped him to the door. "Who the hell was that shooting at you, Barbara?"

"How the hell should I know, David? I'm not the cop here. You are!" Sgt, Vance and Barbara helped Jimmy get into the back of the cruiser. "Mark!" Sgt. Vance shouted. "Get over here, and give Jimmy a ride to the hospital. He's been shot!" Sgt. Vance helped Jimmy into the cruiser and slammed the door. Barbara sat in the back seat. "Jimmy," Barbara said. "Just relax. Mark is going to get us to the hospital, and you'll be fine. Just relax." Jimmy's head dropped back on the seat and his face went white.

"We could just call an ambulance, you know," Mark said angrily.

"Mark, just drive the fuckin' car, okay." Barbara snapped back. "I sure's hell don't need your shit today."

"I just wanted to make that clear, Barbara. That's all. So, how's Richie doing?"

"Fuck off, Mark. That wasn't called for. You know what happened with us." Mark smiled big and wide like he just won the lottery.

"Mom," Jimmy spoke softly. I have something I need to tell you. But I know you're not going to like what I have to say. It's about Leslie."

"Jesus Christ, Jimmy, you're getting a divorce?" She stated rolling her eyes. "More shit to add to the misery."

"No, no, Mom. It's not that, it's something else."

Mark was obviously trying to listen in their conversation. Jimmy looked up and saw Mark's eyes in the rear-view mirror. "I will tell you later about it," he said, tipping his head toward the front of the car. Barbara looked up and saw Mark's eyes staring at her in the mirror.

"Okay, Jimmy," she said calmly.

43

Jimmy rested his shoulder on a pillow in the hospital waiting room with his mother by his side, waiting for the doctor to give the release papers He was still in pain, even though the doctor had given him some Vicodin pain killers. He felt groggy.

"Mom," he said with his eyes closed. "I have something I seriously need to tell you."

"What, Jimmy?" she answered him, looking around to make sure no one could hear them talking. "What is it, Jimmy?" she asked again, and then realized he'd fallen asleep. "Jesus, "she muttered. She saw the doctor who had treated Jimmy coming around the corner and stood out in the hall blocking his way. "I'm sorry, Doctor, but can you tell me when we are allowed to leave?" she asked.

"At this moment, Mrs. Williams, your son needs to stay here. He's not well enough to travel. He's been shot in the shoulder, and we need to see if any nerve damage has been done before he can leave." Barbara rolled her eyes. She knew the doctor was lying, but she knew she couldn't argue with him. "Okay, Doc, but when do you think that will be?"

"There's a cafeteria on the west wing if you want to get a cup of coffee," he told her, ignoring her questions.

"Thank you, but I . . . Never mind then, I'll wait."

The doctor smiled at her and continued walking and staring down at his clipboard. Barbara rolled her eyes again watching him walk away and thought about the coffee. She looked at Jimmy asleep, or unconscious. She had no clue what kind of condition he was in. She felt a tap on the shoulder and turned around to see an older doctor. He was quite tall and rather handsome, she thought, with broad shoulders, a white short cut mustache that matched his short hair, and the usual white doctor's overcoat.

"Hello!" she said, rather surprised. The doctor smiled and peered into the emergency room where her son was sleeping.

"My name is Dr. Voigt." He introduced himself in a strictly professional way. "I have some good news for you, but I also have some bad news. Do you want to talk here, or do you want to talk in the conference room?"

"You have bad news? What kind of bad news?"

Your son has some bone damage in his shoulder. Unfortunately, Jimmy received the bullet in a spot where his shoulder could break if he moves it the wrong way, but if we do an operation and fix the problem, he could take up to six weeks to heal, or even longer." Barbara looked around for a chair to sit in. She didn't think he was in this bad of shape. Now the question popped into her thoughts. "Doctor, how much is this operation going to cost? I don't have any insurance."

"With the way things are, it could cost anywhere between six and ten thousand dollars."

"Jesus, I don't have that kind of money lying around. How much time do I have to get him fixed up?"

"Well, you really don't have a lot of time. But we could put a brace on him to prevent him from moving it the wrong way until you come up with the money. Or you can just let him heal and hope to God he doesn't do anything stupid."

"I'll see what I can do. Thanks for your honesty. Now, when can we go home?"

"Once you're cleared from here, and you're cleared from the police, you can leave."

"Cleared from the police? What do you mean cleared from the police? We haven't done anything wrong. Jimmy's the victim here." Barbara was getting annoyed with the police department and even with this doctor. "I want to go home and finish the day with a hot cup of tea. Is that so much to ask? Jesus Christ, what else is going to happen?" Then she remembered. "So what's the good news?"

"Just that your son is all patched up for the time being."

"Gee, thanks, Doc," She said. Down the hall she saw Sgt. Vance and Officer Mathias with two rent-a-cops walking behind them. "Can you give me something to knock me out?" she asked, only half kidding.

44

"Barbara," Mark spoke. "I'm sorry to tell you this, but we have a warrant for Jimmy's arrest, for the murder of his wife, Leslie Williams. The Anchorage P.D. called this morning and talked to Chief Flynn about Jimmy. They have a nation wide APB out for him as we speak. They knew he had family in here, so they had a good feeling he was going to hide out here." Barbara just looked at Mark dumbfounded.

"Well," she said, then sighed. "He's right there if you want to arrest him." Mark looked at the two rent-a-cops and gestured to them, when suddenly Jimmy jumped out of bed and dashed toward the door. Sgt. Vance yanked out his billy-club in a blink of an eye and snapped it across Jimmy's face. Jimmy fell flat on his back, unconscious. "Handcuff that bastard before he wakes up." Sgt. Vance ordered. The rent-a-cops spun him around and placed handcuffs on his wrists and then carried him down the hallway with his feet dragging on the floor out to the police cruiser. "Barbara, I'm sorry this had to happen." Mark spoke clearly. "But we need to do our job, just like everyone else."

"What happened to the dead body in my yard, David?" Barbara asked.

"Let me guess, was it Roger Cass's crazy mother? She said she wanted revenge on my family for killing her son. Now, I guess she's looking for payment. How did Jimmy kill his wife, David?"

"Barbara, it was pretty gruesome. Not sure you want to know."

"I'm sure it was, considering Leslie was a cold-hearted bitch. I'm surprised he didn't kill her a lot earlier."

"That bad, huh?" Mark asked

"Are you going to tell me how Leslie was killed, or do I have to read it in the newspaper?"

"I'll tell you how, but you're not going to like it. Like I said, Barbara, it's gruesome."

"I can take it."

"He chopped her up with an axe, and then hung her remains all over the woods so the wolves would feed on her. A hunter found all the frozen remains and called the police." Barbara's face blanched.

"Jesus Christ," she said. "I need to sit down. Jesus, I need to sit down."

"Well, you wanted to know, so I told you," Mark said, helping her to a chair.

"I know," Barbara put her head into her hands. "Can somebody please give me a ride home?" she asked him, her forehead moist. "I need to go home. I need to end this god awful day." She got up and walked out to the lobby. The automatic doors

opened, and a rush of cold air hit her.   "Barbara!"
David shouted just before the doors closed behind
her

"Barbara," David calmly took her arm. "I'll
give you a ride home." He walked her to his car.   "I
still need to talk to you about Roger Cass."

"David," she said, slamming the door after
she sat in. "I honestly, truly don't know why that
kid was killed in my yard. I don't have any explan-
ation."

"What about Whitney?"

"She's in love with that kid up the street.
He comes down quite often and stays for hours. He
likes to watch her paint downstairs, so she says.
I think she's downstairs fucking the little bastard
if you ask me. Every time I open the door to
the basement, Whitney's always buttoning up her
shirt."

"Who is this kid up the street?"

"His name is Andy. I can't remember his last
name for some reason, but he hangs around with
that David kid who, I hear is doing or selling drugs
to the other neighborhood kids."

"That would be Luke."

"Luke? Luke who? I've never heard anybody
by the name of Luke."

"Never mind then Barbara, let's just stick
with the murder case. Where does this Andy kid
live?"

"He lives up on South Pleasant Street, on the
corner."

David pulled into Barbara's driveway and saw all the men still walking around the yard. He didn't want to say to much to her, but he figured he could probably lie his way out of it if he needed to.

"I'm going inside for a hot cup of tea," she said, opening the door. David looked behind him and saw Mark pulling up.

"David," Barbara whispered. "Do you want to join me?" David looked at her dumbfounded. "I don't know, Barbara. I need to take care of things before I can sit down and relax, you know." Barbara just nodded her head and went inside. No sooner had she shut the door then felt a hand slam over her mouth with a gun press hard against her temple.

"One little peep you fuckin' bitch and that little whore of a daughter of yours is dead."

45

The intruder looked out the window and saw the police still swarming around the yard. She grinned with her nice white teeth, and then pressed the gun harder to Barbara's temple. "You listen to me, you fuckin' cunt. I don't need any bullshit from you. One bad move and I'll murder you and that slut of a daughter you have. I killed that asshole in your yard because he deserved to die. I had to kill him, and now I'm going to kill you and your fuckin' daughter because my life was ruined when your fuckin' husband killed Peter. Once those pigs out there are done playing fuck-fuck games, you and Whitney can kiss your sorry ass lives goodbye."

"Barbara mumbled something through the assailant's hand. She removed her hand from Barbara's mouth just enough to let her speak. "Who are you?" Barbara asked.

"You know who I am. I'm the person you should be very afraid of, bitch. Now no more questions."

The woman looked out the window again waiting for the police to leave when she heard a door shut upstairs. She looked up, waiting for whoever it was when Barbara bit down hard on her hand.

"Jesus fucking Christ that hurt!" she screamed and let Barbara go. Barbara fell to the floor and crawled as fast as she could toward the kitchen. Suddenly, she felt a kick in the stomach, causing her to throw up her morning coffee. The woman swung the gun high in the air and hit Barbara on the back of the head, knocking her unconscious. She hit her again as hard as she could, noticing the gun barrel impaled her head, and blood drenched Barbara's hair.

"Mom," the assailant heard Whitney say from the top of the steps. She looked up and saw the girl slowly coming down the stairs rubbing her eyes. She picked up Barbara by the arms and dragged her to the kitchen, and then dropped her on the floor.

"Mom?" Whitney called again and came through the kitchen doorway. Whitney gasped at the hooded intruder and felt the hit across her face. She saw stars when her head hit the floor. She remembered Peter slapping her in the face, and his class ring cutting the bridge of her nose. Suddenly, Whitney felt a gun barrel digging into her temple. "I'm going to kill you, you fuckin' whore" The voice was loud yet definitely feminine. "If it wasn't for you, Peter would still be alive and in my arms where he belongs." Whitney felt another thump across her face. Her right eye shut. She was certain she was going to be dead soon.

Whitney looked at the woman hovering over, holding the gun. She glanced at her mother, lying motionless on the floor, blood covering the side of her head. She could give up and die quickly, or she could fight one more time. She quickly whipped her legs around with a smooth karate chop, and flipped the assailant's legs out from under her, watching her land flat on her back. Whitney jumped to her feet ninja-style, and kicked the gun away from the killer's hand. She stomped on her chest as hard as she could, trying to knock the wind out of her, and then kicked her in the face. Whitney repeatedly kicked at the masked face until she saw blood oozing from the black winter face mask. She reached down and ripped it off to see who the killer was. She was surprised to see it was the strange, quiet girl who lived next to the Wallace's boatyard.

"Ashley Tufts, you stupid bitch!" She said out loud. "Why!" She screamed at the top of her lungs. "Why!" she screamed again and dropped to her knees to the floor. She knew Ashley was dead. She had kicked her to death. She killed her trying to save her own life. Whitney looked at her mother still motionless and crawled over to her. Barbara's eyes were wide open, her blood puddled on the floor. "Mom," Whitney cried. "Mom," she said again and heard the front door open.

"Barbara!" Sgt. Vance yelled, slamming the door. He hurried into the kitchen and saw Whitney leaning over her mother, holding her head on her lap. "David, please help me!" Whitney cried. "Please help me!" David pulled the radio from his belt and shouted to dispatch for an ambulance. He quickly went over to Barbara and felt her neck for a pulse. "She's still with us, Whitney," he said with relief. "She's alive. Who the hell is this?" he asked, pointing to Ashley. They heard the front door open, and several officers ran into the kitchen with their guns drawn.

"She's Ashley Tufts," Whitney replied, wiping her eyes. "She lives down next to the boatyard. I think she's dead."

"Who killed her, Whit?"

"I did, David. She was going to kill me! Look at my face!" She shouted in hysterics. "She was going to kill me, David!"

"This is going to be one long fuckin' day." David said, shaking his head. Whitney touched her face and felt the pain and tenderness of her skin. Her new pajama top covered with small butterflies was ripped at the collar, and her hair was knotted with blood.

"Are you all right, Whitney?" David asked calmly. Whitney started crying even more. She couldn't stop. "No," she answered, stroking her mother's hair. The paramedics came in holding a big tackle box filled with medical equipment and a stretcher. David put his hand out to Whitney to help her off the floor. Whitney touched his hand and began to cry even harder. She stood up and put her arms around David, pressing her face damaged against his shoulder.

"Everything is going to be all right, Whitney. Everything is going to be all right."

46

I woke up after a restless night, hearing the wind howling in every direction. Downstairs my mother was talking on the telephone. I grabbed the orange juice from the refrigerator, listening to my mother's conversation. . Then I heard my mother mention the Williams, and I stopped what I was doing with my back toward her. She said it again, Williams. I turned my head toward my mother wondering what the hell was happening. I heard her say goodbye to who ever she was talking to and lightly hung up the phone.

"What's going on?" I asked. As usual, my mother shook her head, said nothing and then went into the living room to sit down in her usual spot on the couch. I took a big gulp of my orange juice walking into the living room and placed my glass on the antique dining room table.   "What happened?" I asked her again.

"What did David do with that golden sword you stole from the old house across the river?" she asked, casually picking up her crochet needles.

"I don't know, why?"

"Well, because Roger Cass was killed with it

last night."

"What? Are you serious? Where did he get killed?" I asked, thinking maybe someone broke into his house and finally did him in as everyone in the neighborhood wanted.

"In front of your so-called girlfriend's house. So, what did David do with that sword?"

"I don't know, why?"

"Because, that's what Roger Cass was killed with," She said again, but only this time it was with a nasty attitude. I was completely shocked. David couldn't have killed him.   "Mom," I said quietly. "Did David kill him?" My mother dropped the crochet needles to her lap and looked at me straight in the eye.

"No," she said and breathed a sigh of relief. "The girl that lives next to Wallace's boatyard did. What's her name? The tall girl that always looks so thin."

"Are you talking about Ashley Tufts?"

I went back into the kitchen and poured myself another glass of orange juice and started to think about everything. "Man, talk about bad luck." I said out loud.

"David called. He said he'll be down later!" My mother yelled.

"What time?" I replied, and then heard the door shut.

"He's here now."

"Hey," David said, walking into the kitchen. "You gonna pour me a glass?"

"Pour your own glass. You know where they are."

"Gee, thanks, asshole," he said and reached for a glass. He grabbed the orange juice, spilling a little on the counter, and then sucked it up with his mouth like a vacuum cleaner.

I walked back into the living room to finish talking to my mother about the Whitney's family. David followed me and sat down on the couch closest to the fireplace filled with paper and logs.

"So, Whitney is in the hospital," Mom continued. "Her mother is in a coma and could very well pass away, and her brother is in jail for murdering his wife." My mouth fell open. I looked at David, and he looked at me as though he could really give a shit.

"Where did you put the golden sword, David?" My mother asked.

"I gave it to Ashley Tuft's father because he liked it when I was walking by his house the day you told me to get rid of it."

"Well, that's just great. Now we know where Ashley got the sword."

"Do you want me to get the sword back?" David asked.

"David, you can't. The sword was used as a murder weapon." David looked at me dumbfounded.

"Roger Cass was killed last night," I explained.

"Andy, there is one other thing I haven't told you yet. That girl Ashley, she was also killed last night."

"Wow, that's messed up. Mom, how did you get all this information? Who were you talking to?" My mother shook her head.

"Your god-awful father called. He told me everything because apparently, he was down there as a paramedic. He told me Whitney said your name more than just once, so he assumed you two were dating.

"Is that what's going on with you and her?" she asked.

"No," I said. "We're just friends. That's all." I started sweating like there was no tomorrow. I needed to leave the house quick, but unfortunately I was still in my pajamas. "I need to go get dressed. I'll be down in a minute. What do you want to do today, David?"

"I got my bike outside. You wanna ride uptown?" David asked, knowing I didn't have a leg to stand on at this point.

"Sure," I said, rolling my eyes. "What the fuck?" I whispered under my breath as I was walking upstairs. What I wanted to do was rush to the hospital and hold Whitney in my arms. Suddenly the phone rang. "I got it!" I yelled. I picked the phone up in my sister's room on the second ring. "Hello," I said with a loud voice.

"Andy?" A girl's voice asked. It was Cheater, the famous town crier.

"Cheater?" I asked, wondering if it indeed was her, even though I knew it was.

"Yeah, it's me."

"What now?" I replied with an attitude, thinking she's got some more bullshit news she's made up about Whitney. Or, I thought, was she going to reiterate everything I just heard about Whitney's family?

"Andy, I think I'm pregnant, and the last person I was with was you.

47

I felt light headed. I started sweating profusely and felt the sweat pouring down my face. I had to quickly kneel down on the floor before I fell. I felt the rug against my face. I lay flat on my stomach breathing faster and faster, almost to the point of hyperventilating. I couldn't think. I couldn't listen. I couldn't do anything but lay on the floor, feeling the strands from the rug itch my face.

"Andy?" Cheater said ever so softly. I didn't say anything, I couldn't. I started feeling like I was actually crying. "Andy?" she said again. I lifted my face off the rug and sat up on my knees. I wiped my face feeling the marks the rug left and wiped away the tears of foreboding.

"What?" I asked Cheater. I slowed my breathing and stroked my hand hard across the top of my head. I didn't want to talk to her anymore, but the truth had to be told between us.

"Are you sure you're pregnant?" I asked her again. There was a long pause over the phone

"Well, I'm not, actually. But I just wanted to call you and see what you would say if I actually was because I've been thinking about having one." My mouth dropped to the floor.

"You are a fucking douche-bag!" I screamed at the top of my lungs. "How could you, you fucking skank!" I hung up the phone; actually, I slammed it down and broke the button on the base. "Aahh, I hate you!" I screamed again.

"Andrew Peter!" my mother shouted from downstairs. "There will be no swearing in this house!" David came running up the stairs wondering what was going on. I told him Cheater just totally pissed me off by lying to me that she was pregnant, and I was the father. David's eyes widened, and his mouth dropped. "You fucked her?" he asked with total surprise. I looked at him. He looked as though he was ready to fight. I was caught between a rock and a hard place. Do I lie? Or do I tell the truth at the same time he punches me in the face. "I went to her house one day with her, after I stopped over at Whitney's. She wanted to play, so I did."

"Yeah, well, you didn't know Whitney was fucking someone else other than you, did you?" I started feeling another panic attack coming on. Again, the heavy breathing started, the sweats, the dizziness. I sat down on the bed. I looked at David ready to faint to the floor. "Whitney has another boyfriend?" I asked.

"Yup," he answered with a shit-eaten grin on his face.

"Who is it?" I tried to sift through the

names in the neighborhood. I thought of two boys whom she thought were cute at the first dance of the school year, and then I remembered Jonathan's friend whom we don't see very often. I quickly remembered Whitney commenting on how sexy he looked in his football uniform. He had a nice body, she said. He was so muscular. Jason Rossi was his name. He was quiet, and somewhat secretive. He'd sneak around with women much older than he was, even the married women. He worked as a gardener during high school, and we figured the quick roll in the hay was part of his payment. Every now and then, David and I would walk the neighborhood, and we would see the bright green rake Jason would use leaning against the doorway. It's funny that he never did get caught all those times "It's friggin' Jason Rossi, isn't it?" I asked David, catching my breath again.

"Jason's still in New York. Why would he be down here?"

"Two words," I said. "Spring-break" David's lying to me again for the hundredth time, I thought. But David shook his head, still smiling.

"Who is it then?" I demanded.

"Dude, I'm just kidding around with you. Relax, there is no one else," he said and breathed a heavy sigh.

"You're an asshole. Just like Cheater." I walked into my room. I jumped on my bed and lay my head on my pillow. "Go home, David," I said. "Just fuckin leave. I don't need your shit anymore." David stared at me expressionless. "Fine then, dick. I'll be uptown if you're looking for me." He went down the steps, and slammed the door behind him.

Everything was peaceful and quiet for a long while. I almost fell asleep, until the phone rang. I ran over and picked it up. It was Whitney. She was calling from the hospital. Her mother was dead.

48

I sat on the top step listening to her tale of everything that had happened that morning and how Ashley had killed her mother. Whitney could barely speak out the words. She also told me what happened to her brother Jimmy.

I was in shock. I was speechless. Suddenly, the phone went dead. I didn't even hear her say good-bye. All I heard was a faint click, and then nothing. I knew she would likely go downstairs to her basement studio and paint, just as she had when her father killed himself.

"Mom," I yelled down the stairs.

"What is it, Andrew?" she answered.

"Whitney's mom is dead," I told her and rested my head against the wall. I thought about David, and wondered if he was still uptown with that shitbag dope smoker.

"What?" my mother spoke louder. "What happened now?"

"Ashley Tufts killed her." I could sense my mother was shaking her head in disappointment. She had that habit of doing so. She never really said much when things went wrong. Then again, she never really did care for the Williams family anyway.

"How did she kill her?" My mother asked.

"I don't know, Mom," I said and went down the stairs where she was sitting. I sat down on the other couch. "I'm glad it's Saturday," I said. "I didn't feel like going to school anyway."

"I said this once before a long time ago. Some-day there's going to be no one left alive in that Williams family," my mother said.

"Well, I'm going to find David." What I really wanted to do was go down to the smashed in mail-boxes and throw a rock at Cheater's head. I got up off the couch and went upstairs to get dressed, grabbed my boots and coat and ran back down-stairs to the front door. When I opened it, there was David, standing on my front steps.

"Hey," he said. "You still mad at me?"

"No," I lied. "What's the matter?" He looked as though he had seen a ghost.

"Dude," he whispered so my mother wouldn't hear him. "You should see what's going on down at Whitney's."

"What now?" I asked, wondering what else could possibly happen.

"There's so much blood down there, and the cops, the ambulance, fire trucks. I even saw your dad there. You have to go down and see."

"Mom, I'll be home later," I told her and walked out the door.

"Did you see Cheater looking out the window? I want to smash her head in for what she said this morning."

"Yeah, I did. She's nothing but a waste of a perfectly good chick. She's fun to play with, though." David had to reiterate that, since he lost his membership from her.

We managed to make it down to Whitney's house and stood across the street in the old lady's driveway. We watched for a long while, noting all the blood in the driveway. Then suddenly, the front door opened up. The paramedic's walked out holding a stretcher with a bright orange body bag on top. "That's Ashley Tufts in that bag, I bet," David commented. "She's the one that killed Whitney's mother."

"How do you know all that?" I asked.

"Easy, I overheard the cops talking about it the first time I was here." We stood and watched the orange bag slide into the back of the ambulance and looked at all the police still swarming the house like bees in the middle of the summer. "Sgt. Vance is staring at us. We better split," David said and started walking toward the church.

"Where are you going, David?" Sgt. Vance yelled. David stopped and looked at Vance walking toward us. "Nowhere, Sarg," David replied. "What do you want with me?" he asked.

"I want to ask you some questions. That's all, and you too, Andy. I want to talk to you about the murder weapon that was used."

"What murder weapon?" David spoke defensively, "I don't know anything about no murder weapon."

"Gee, David, nothing like making yourself guilty," Sgt Vance sneered. "What's your story, Mr. Andy? Whitney's mom said you and Whitney are quite the couple. Where did the sword come from?" I stood there feeling intimidated. I looked around at all the police cars, fire trucks, ambulance, and of course, the coroner's heap of a vehicle, a 1961 black Cadillac with rot around the wheel wells. "I don't know anything about a golden sword." I said. David rolled his eyes at me. He knew I slipped up.

"How did you know it was gold?" Sgt. Vance spoke.

"All swords are gold." I lied trying to squeeze my way out of this bullshit. "Me and David got to go. We need to go uptown to get something to eat," I said looking for an escape.

"I don't think either of you are going anywhere until you tell me about the sword."

"Sarg, we picked up the sword from the old abandoned house across the river," David explained. "We didn't know it was going to be used as a murder weapon. Christ, we didn't think anything at all. Andy's Mom told me to get rid of it, so I gave it to Mr. Tufts."

"So, you broke into the house across the river?" Sarg Vance asked, wondering if there was anything else valuable in there that the police should confiscate.

"What's up with Jimmy, Sarg?" I asked already knowing about his wife being murdered. I just wanted to shift the conversation to something not concerning us.

"That's something I can't talk about. What else can you tell me about this Roger Cass?"

"He was an asshole, and I'm glad he's dead," David said.

"He was looking to kill Whitney because of Peter," I added. He stalked her all the time ever since Whitney's father killed his brother." Sgt Vance turned around and watched the movement in the yard.

"Go away you too. Go away from this place." Sarg Vance said. David and I went up the street and came to the smashed in mailboxes. I looked at Cheater's bedroom window and didn't see her standing there with her regular tank top on with no bra. I told myself I was going to settle the score with her, and I meant it. "I'm going to talk to Meredith for a minute. I'll be right back." David rolled his eyes at me again, which I really was starting to get annoyed with. "I'll meet you uptown," he told me, and started to leave. When David wasn't looking, I flipped him the bird.

I knocked on Cheater's door and looked at David still heading toward town. The door swung open, and Cheater stood there with her eyes all puffy from crying. "What's the matter now?" I asked. She looked at me. "I told Ashley, I wanted Roger Cass dead in the worst way, but everything went very wrong. Now Whitney's mom is dead, and it's my fault. I didn't think Ashley was going to kill Roger and Whitney's mom. She's crazy, she's fuckin' really crazy."

Cheater put her face down in her hands. She was looking for me to wrap my arms around her, but I didn't dare to touch her. Cheater basically put a hit out on Roger Cass, and Ashley took it upon herself to carry out the mission. "Come in, Andy. Please come in. It's cold out there," she said, moving away from the door. I walked in, and then I heard the sound of the phone. Cheater ran over and picked it up on the first ring. "Hello," she said quietly. "Are you okay, Whitney? I'm really worried about you. Andy's here with me." Suddenly, my heart started pounding like crazy. I felt dizzy. I couldn't breathe right. I quickly went to go sit down, but the closest place I could sit was the staircase. My knees went to the floor before I made it to the stairs, and then my face landed on the floor hard. Cheater looked at me and smiled, not knowing the fact that she just told Whitney I was here, and the only thing Whitney was going to hear was, I'm going to tag Cheater. "Yeah, me and Andy are going upstairs to hang out in my room." I heard Cheater say. "Hello, Whitney. Are you still there? The phone just went dead, Andy. I don't know what happened."

"I know what happened, Cheater. You just signed my death certificate." I think I fainted after that because I woke up naked in Cheater's bed.

49

Three months later the snow was gone and leaves were popping out on the trees. I walked passed Whitney's house trying not to stare at her window. I looked in her yard where her dog was tied up and saw Whitney painting in her usual spot. I watched her from a distance, remembering the way things use to be, her smell, her soft touch, her beautiful long silky hair. I closed my eyes for moment thinking about her perfume lingering around me. I breathed in, holding a smile, when suddenly I opened my eyes and saw her. "Shit," I whispered. I started walking down the hill toward the church. I felt her eyes burning in the back of me, watching, possibly wanting to kill. I knew from the way she looked at me, things between us were very tense.

"You're nothing but a friggin' unsympathetic prick!" she screamed at me. I turned around and looked at her.

"I didn't have anything to do with your mother's death!" I shouted back. God only knows why I even said that, but it had to be said I guess. Whitney walked back to her painting still staring at me while she picked up her brush. I continued on past the church toward Wallace's boatyard, steaming in my head about her I heard the rumbling noise of Jonathan's truck coming up the street from where Randy lives. He stopped in front of me and slid the cigarette from the back of his ear into his mouth and lit it. "What's going on?" he asked, sucking a drag. I saw Tweedle Dotz in the truck close to the window, crying. "Not much. Just got yelled at by Whitney," I said.

"Dude, fuck her, she ain't worth shit. Besides, that Aunt Sarah of hers, is a no good bitch. Christ, she won't even let Whitney out of the house." I didn't understand what he was talking about because I had no idea who Whitney's aunt was. He explained that her aunt moved in to take care of things. "Get in," he said. "We're going to have some beers at the pits." He didn't ask me if I wanted to go. He just said "get in," so I did, and I was excited to sit next to Dotz.

I felt the power of the truck when Jonathan stepped on the gas, and off we flew. He drove by Whitney's house and pressed the horn. We just stared at each other as we drove by. I thought I saw her flip me the bird, but it was only her brush slamming against the canvas. Then Jonathan had the nerve to drive by Cheater's house even slower. We all looked over, and there she was, stretched out in a lawn chair with a bikini on. Her stomach was flat as a pancake. God, she was gorgeous. I couldn't stop staring at her. "She had an abortion,"

Dotz said. "Rumor has it, it was your kid."

"Yeah, I suppose it was," I agreed. Jonathan managed to drive through the bump path into the pits. I saw Randy's Blazer parked just about horizontally on the sand pile. He was leaning against the back drinking a beer, and talking to what appeared to be his nephew, Jason Rossi. I crouched down, hoping he didn't see me and start giving me shit about Whitney. You know, the old, 'I told you so' speech.

We parked near Randy's truck. I opened the door and at the same time, I felt Dotz's hand grab my arm. I looked at her. She was still filled with tears.

"What's the matter?" I asked her and rubbed my thumb across her cheek wiping the tears away. "Jonathan has been telling everyone about how Whitney should have died with her mother. I don't want to be around him anymore, but he still forces me and Deanna to be with him any chance he gets." I looked over at Jonathan talking with Randy and Jason, and I got the urge to go over there and punch him in the face. I looked inside the back of the truck and grabbed the closest thing I could reach, a long one and a half inch Craftsman wrench. I walked toward Jonathan, holding the wrench like a weapon, and whipped it right into the lower part of his back. Jonathan dropped to his knees. I hit him again in the back of the head, and then watched him drop to the sand. "That'll teach you to fuckin' talk about Whitney like that, asshole!" I shouted. I dropped the wrench to the ground and walked away toward the road.

Randy and Jason just stood there in shock. I kept walking. I didn't even look back. I could not have cared less what that black bastard had to say until I heard his truck starting up. I looked back and saw Dotz jump out of the truck and watched as Jonathan came closer with a cloud of dust pouring from the rear tires. He drove straight toward me, determined to run me over. I ran as fast as I could to the woods and jumped behind a big maple tree. Jonathan kept coming fast and furious. I looked at him from around the maple tree, and then dashed further into the woods.

Jonathan crashed the front of his truck into the tree I was hiding behind. Everything became suddenly quiet and still. Then the truck exploded. I ran to it and grabbed Jonathan by the T-shirt. I yanked him out of the truck, dragged him away as far as I could. "I'm still going to kill you for hitting me," he said, blood covering his face.

I dropped him down on the sand and stared at him. "At least I saved your sorry ass life," I told him and walked away. Just when I got to the end of the sand pit, I saw stars, dropped to my knees, and felt my face hit the dirt.

50

I awoke with a nasty headache. When I my eyes finally focused, I was lying face down in a quagmire. My clothes were covered in thick black mud; I couldn't even lift my head, it hurt so bad. I guess who ever hit me left the wrench next to my right shoulder to remind me of how much of an asshole I was. I guess I deserved it, considering Jonathan's truck blew up.

I managed to struggle out of the mud and scuffed my feet back down the trail toward the sand pile. I felt the back of my head and felt the blood almost dried to my hair and the cut where the wrench hit me. As I was walking, I wondered if Jonathan hit me, or Randy, or Jason helping Jonathan.

I looked around the sand pit. I was alone. They all just left me lying in the mud. I looked at Jonathan's truck still smoking like a wood pile and turned around and headed down the trial to get the hell home. I walked past Whitney's house almost four hours later, still dizzy from getting hit. I saw Whitney still painting in her usual spot, and painting the usual painting. She looked at me from the corner of her eye, and then turned her head. She didn't say anything. I continued walking home but I had to stop at the mailboxes to rest.

"You should have someone look at that," I heard behind me.

"I know," I said. Cheater sat next to me staring at the blood on my head. "She hit you good."

"She?" I questioned. "What do you mean, she?"

"Yeah, I was told Dotty was the one who smacked you with the crowbar."

"It was a wrench," I corrected her.

"Whatever. She hit you nice and hard."

"Why the fuck did she hit me? She was the one who told me she was frightened by Jonathan, and she was the one that told me Jonathan was spreading shit around, about how Whitney should have died with her mother." I started getting upset again, but it only made my head hurt more.

"Come on, I'll get you cleaned up," Cheater said and got up. I looked at her wondering if she was really going to clean me up or was she going to tag me for the third time. "Get up," she said. "I'm not going to bite you."

"Why not, everyone else seems to want to," I said, rubbing my head. "I hate this neighborhood with a passion."

"Come on. Stop yelling, and let's go."

I sat at the kitchen table facing the window,

with a towel wrapped around my neck. I felt awkward sitting there like I was getting a hair cut, but instead, Cheater was dabbing my head with a wet face cloth. "It's not as bad you think it is," she commented. "But man, she hit you good."

"Why the hell did she hit me, is what I want to know?"

"Because she saw you hit Jonathan, who is her boyfriend, duh. You didn't know that? She set you up. She wanted to know what you would do if she told you about the rumor."

"Speaking of rumors, did you have an abortion?"

"No, I had a miscarriage."

"Who got you pregnant?"

"You did." My heart sank to my feet. I felt light-headed and dizzy. I wanted to lie down, but I was afraid if I did, I'd wake up naked again.

"Here, have some aspirin and some water. This should make your head feel better. I went to grab the water from her hand and leaned forward against her. Next thing I knew, I woke up lying on the couch with a blanket around me. I looked around wondering what happened, and then looked under the blankets. I still had my clothes on.

I tossed the blanket to my feet and slowly sat up. My head still hurt so bad, I thought it was going to explode. "Hello, asshole," I heard Whitney say, sitting in the recliner. I looked at her with my eyes still blurry. I didn't say anything.

"Why didn't you come to my mother's funeral and support me?" she asked angrily.   "I didn't think you wanted me near you, after what happened."

"So, what did happen between you and Cheater?" she asked and pressed her teeth together hard.

"Nothing happened between us, Whitney," Cheater quickly interrupted. "It was David. He was the one who got me pregnant. Not him." I looked at Cheater, thinking she just lied for me to get me out of this mess. I then looked at Whitney wondering if she was going to buy that. She did.

"I'm going home," I said and got up. I walked to the door and put my hand on the handle expecting Whitney to come over and grab me. She didn't.

I walked in my house, and saw my mother sitting on the couch. She looked at me covered in dried mud. She shook her head as usual and breathed a heavy sigh. "Were you playing football again at the park?" she asked.

"Yeah," I said and went upstairs to my room. I took off my clothes and lay down on my bed thinking about what had happened, and then fell asleep.

51

Summer and fall just seemed to race by. I didn't see anybody after the day Jonathan's truck went up in flames. No one called. No one came over, not even David. He was obviously hanging around with that shitbag on River Road, smoking pot, and whatever else he'd been doing. I just stayed home and worked out in the yard, raking leaves, mowing the lawn. Occasionally, I would walk down to Wallace's boatyard and go fishing for a couple of hours.

I often would think about life and wonder where it was going to take me. Sometimes I would just fall asleep in the sun with my line out in the water and forget about everything for a while. I needed to be alone, to think, to wonder, and to breathe.

Then the strangest thing happened. I came home from walking through the woods in a place David and I called a forest on a hill that over looked the river, Old Smokey. The pine trees were tall, and there was a cliff at the edge of the forest, overlooking River Road. When I was younger I often thought the tops of the pine trees touched the clouds.

Anyway, when I came home, I saw Whitney sitting out on the patio chair with her hands tucked inside her gray sweatshirt. It was a little cold that day for a mid October afternoon.

I sat in the chair across from her without saying a word. We sat there in silence, looking at each other. I was afraid to say anything, fearing she'd come all unglued, and start screaming at me. She closed her eyes for a moment, and then covered her head with the hood on her sweatshirt. She did look as though she'd lost a little weight, but after all the shit she's gone through that wouldn't be surprising.

"What's going on?" I asked finally.

"I'm leaving," she said and got up off the chair. "You broke the silence." She walked away, around the house and down the path to the street. I raised my arms in the air in frustration, and then walked into my house. I wondered why she showed up, but then again, I guess I really didn't care one way or another. Things got boring after that. Day by day, week after week, school sucked more as time went by. None of my friends came around. Even in high school they pretty much forgot about me until one day in late November, I heard the phone ringing. It was David. He said Sewer Lane was frozen solid, and we needed to go down and see if we could float on the ice. I was surprised he called and excited.

David came down with his father's waders

on. They looked too small for him. He must've grown taller over the summer, again. "What's up?" he asked.

"Nothing, I guess," I said, and walked down the stairs and out the door. We walked down the street, heading toward Sewer Lane. We passed the mailboxes and looked at Cheater's window to see if she was there. Then we passed Whitney's house. There was a new car in the driveway, a blue Chevy Suburban with chrome wheels and duel exhaust. I figured it must belong to that aunt of hers. I looked up at Whitney's window. I saw her sitting in her white chair.

David and I didn't talk much as we walked. He knew everything about what happened with Jonathan, his truck, Cheater getting knocked up, and me getting hit. He heard it all from the town crier, and also Tweedle Dotz.

Sewer Lane was totally frozen. I didn't think it had been that cold enough out to freeze. David walked down the embankment holding onto the small trees and stepped on the ice. He pressed down harder to see if it would break, and if we could move it around. Then suddenly he fell through the ice. He caught himself with the old log that had fallen some time ago near the bridge. He grabbed the log and pulled himself out with a broken stem of a branch, and then sat down on it. "I'm glad I have my waders on," he said with a slight laugh.

"You okay?" I asked him. I slid down

the embankment and stopped at the log. I looked at David; still somewhat surprised he fell through and laughed with him. I walked and slipped toward the center of the brook, wondering if I'd fall through too. I saw David walking behind me still laughing and sliding toward the bridge, when we heard someone calling our names. We looked up and saw Cheater and Whitney standing at the edge of the bridge looking down at us. Whitney looked sexy in her long black coat that matched her silky hair.

"I thought you couldn't come down here," I shouted.

"My aunt let me go for a walk with Meredith," she shouted back.

"How long are you guys gonna be down there?" Cheater asked. I looked at David.

"We just got here," David yelled.

"Hey, can we go back the way we were?" Whitney shouted at me. I looked up at her, trying to get closer to the bridge. "What do you mean?" I asked. Whitney stepped closer to the edge.

"I mean, can we be a couple again, you and me? Like the way we were before my mom died? I still love you." My heart was racing. I wanted to run up there and grab her and hold her forever. My hands started sweating inside my gloves.

I walked toward the side of the brook. I was going to get up there on the bridge and kiss her. I could already feel her sweet lips on mine. Then I heard Cheater say to her, "Why don't you go down on the ice and give him a kiss?" I looked up and saw Cheater push Whitney against the shoulder. Whitney lost her balance and leaned forward. She threw her arms in the air, and screamed as she tumbled off the bridge. She landed face down on the log. The broken stem of the branch impaled her chest. Whitney was dead. Her hand had crashed through the ice near the spot where David climbed out. Her head rested on the log. Her eyes were open, facing me. I saw a small tear sliding down her nose. I started to cry, I started to shake. I looked up at Cheater standing on the edge of the bridge. She stood there looking down at Whitney, as though she was watching the wind blowing the snow around from her bedroom window.

I grabbed Whitney, and tried to pull her off the log, but I couldn't. She was stuck on the branch that held her. Blood was everywhere on the ice, the log, on my boots. I cried hard, and leaned down touching her cheek with my lips.

"Whitney, get up!" I yelled. "Please, get up!" I knew she was dead. I knew before I even touched her. I knew when she was pushed by Cheater. I knew. "Go call an ambulance!" I yelled. "Go!" David had climbed up the embankment and was running to the nearest house before I even yelled. He knew there was no saving her. He knew there was no more Whitney. I dropped to my knees crying like crazy. I couldn't help her. I wanted to kiss her and bring her back, but I knew miracles just didn't happen; I kissed her on the lips feeling the blood around her mouth.

"They're coming!" David yelled. "I can hear the sirens, Andy! They're coming!" David ran back down the embankment. He looked at Whitney and touched her neck. He couldn't feel a pulse. He pulled his hand away and looked at Cheater still standing there. "You killed her! You killed Whitney! You fuckin' killed Whitney, Cheater!" David stared at her with rage.

"David," I said softly. "It's not worth it. Whitney's gone. There's no way to bring her back." The police came to a sliding stop on the bridge, with the Fire and Rescue truck. Sgt Vance slid down the embankment and saw David and me sitting on the ice next to Whitney. "Get away from her!" he shouted.

"She's dead." David said.

"What happened?" Sgt Vance asked, touching her neck. He then saw the branch sticking out of her back, and quickly stood up. "I suppose she is," he said and sighed. "Now tell me what happened." David looked at me. I could see in his eyes he wanted to tell him the reason she's dead was because the bitch standing on the bridge pushed her. He wanted to tell him Cheater was the killer. "Whitney lost her balance and fell of the bridge, sir," David said. I was surprised. I was in shock. I looked at him through the tears in my eyes. Sgt Vance looked at me.

"Well, is that what happened?" I nodded my head yes. I don't know why I did, but I did.

"Yes, sir. She lost her footage and slipped off the bridge and landed on the log," I said and started crying again. I loved her more than anything in the world.

Sgt. Vance looked up at Meredith who now had tears in her eyes. She nodded her head and fell to her knees, covering her face in her hands. I put my head down on my knees. I couldn't bear to look at Whitney any longer.

"You two, get off the ice," Sgt Vance ordered. "It's not safe for you anymore. You're too big to be doing this shit. Get off the ice." I got up and walked up the embankment holding on the small trees. When I got to the top, I looked down one more time at Whitney. I could see the branch sticking out of her back. It made me sick. I wanted to throw up. I wanted to faint. David looked at me, and then looked at Cheater. "I'm going home, Andy," he said. I looked at him and nodded my head. I watched him walk away from the tragedy. I saw him walk away from our childhood years. I watched him walk away from our friendship.

52

Every year on November fifteenth, I visit the Locust Street Cemetery to visit Whitney. She was buried next to her father and mother. The grave stone reads, Beloved William Family. With Dad the day and year he died. Next it reads Mom, and then Whitney, Beloved daughter, killed by nature. I guess her aunt had a way with words.

It's been fifteen years now since the day she died. I talk to her about what's going on in the neighborhood and pick the weeds around the stone. I place roses on top of the stone and wipe the tears from my cheek. David came with me a couple times.

We never returned to Sewer Lane. We never even talked about it. We never mentioned the fact that Cheater killed her. I rarely saw Cheater at all since then. Not even looking out the window when I drove by to go to work. I heard she married a man from West Newbury, and then two years later, she divorced him when she found out he was having an affair with the next door neighbor. The Cheater got cheated on. How ironic is that? She moved back to her mother's house and I heard she's still there, alone. She never did thank David and me for saving her own life that day. She never said a word. She could have spent the rest of her life behind bars like Whitney's brother, Jimmy. I heard through the grapevine that he was killed by an inmate. That didn't bother me. He deserved whatever he got.

David was still smoking the funny looking cigarettes, and then I heard he graduated to cocaine. I didn't see him very much after Whitney died. He decided to hang around with that shitbag on River Road and get into trouble.

David quit school two years after transferring to Whittier Vo-Tech in Haverhill, Mass. I heard he got arrested in Amesbury a few times for possession of a controlled substance, driving after suspension, and other related charges. He didn't call me anymore. When he got married, he didn't invite me to his wedding. I never met his wife, but I heard there was trouble with their relationship even before they got married.

I was working at a pizza joint trying to make ends meet when David came in on a Tuesday afternoon. We talked for a while about what was going on. I asked him if he wanted to go out and have some beers, shoot the shit, and just hang out. He agreed, smiled at me, grabbed his sub and walked out without paying. I covered the cost, grinning as I put the money in the register.

I left at eleven that night, and went to my apartment where I lived with my wife and two small kids. At three in the morning, I woke up to go deliver the Boston Globe around town. I stopped at the cemetery to take a break, and munch down some honey buns, and drink some strawberry milk. I looked around the cemetery thinking about Whitney and searched for her stone. Then I saw something strange at the flag pole near the small road that wound around the stones. I got out of the car and walked over. It became clearer the closer I got that it was a body I was seeing, hanging from the flag pole with the rope wrapped numerous times around its neck. My breath left me, and I sped up to see if the person was dead. That's when I saw that it was my friend David hanging there. He was dead. I ran back to my car and drove down to the police department. After filling them in on my find, I continued delivering the paper until I was finished. I put it out of my mind. I didn't think about him until my mother called that evening and said there had been a death in town.

"Who is it?" I asked. I knew exactly who it was, but somehow I felt that if I didn't acknowledge it, it wouldn't be true. She paused for a moment and said "David." I felt the room spin, and I fell to the floor. I couldn't breathe. I couldn't feel anything. "Mom, I'll talk to you later," I gasped and hung up the phone. I began to cry. I put my hands against my face. It was as if Whitney had died all over again. My wife came home with the kids and saw me on the floor. She already heard the news from my mother. She kneeled down and put her arms around me,

We went to the funeral, and I saw everyone there. I heard whispering, and some bullshit from Jonathan's mouth. I saw David's father. I looked at him, and my eyes filled with tears. "I don't know what to say," I told him. David's father looked at me and pointed his finger in my face. "You don't say anything," he growled. I walked away and saw David lying in the cherry wood casket. I turned and left.

I didn't go to work for a week after that. I lay on my bed feeling as though I was falling. Everything in my head was a mess. I felt selfish, angry, resentful. I got up and took off on my motorcycle I just restored up to the White Mountains to clear my head.

I came home hours later. My wife and kids were home, and they needed me. I went back to work, but I was still not coping well.

My wife suggested I talk to someone about it. "No!" I screamed at her. This became a regular pattern. I'd find myself breathless, shaking, and depressed. "Go see someone!" my wife would plead. "No!" I'd yell and bang my fist into the wall. I began thinking about suicide. "Go get help!" my wife hollered at me one night, then locked herself in the bathroom, afraid of my rages. I looked at the bathroom door and leaned against it. "Okay," I said.

It took four months for me to realize that David's death was a start of my own nervous breakdown. I simply couldn't accept the fact that my best friend was dead, my brother, killed by his own hands.

I ran into Jonathan at a funeral for one of our friend's dad. He smiled at me but seemed reluctant to acknowledge me. I nodded my head and continued to move with the line. After I made it outside, he came to me and held his hand out. I took his hand and tears filled my eyes. He wrapped his arm around me. "I'll talk to you sometime soon," he said, and walked away. Some years later, I drove a new red truck into Jonathon's driveway. He was sitting in a lawn chair talking to Randy when he saw me.

"I came to pay you back for your old truck. I know it was my fault it blew up, so I wanted to give you this." For the first time in his life, Jonathan had nothing to say. He just smiled and patted me on the back.

END.